First Edition, Green Day Press, June 2008

Published in the United States by Green Day Press, a division of The Odes Media Company, New York, New York. Originally published by Ricardo Campesino in Havana in 1959 when Che and Fidel where marching soldiers back and forth past reporters in the Sierra Maestra.

Library of Congress Cataloging-in-Publication Data
Cabrera, Felipe, 1927-1998
An American Fury/ by Ernesto Guerrero : Edited by Big PaPa BRUCE.
ISBN 978-0-6152-2285-1
I. Title. II. Series.
PR6019.09U4 2008
832′.912—dc20 89-40555
CIP

Printed in the mountains of the Sierra Maestra out of green capitalist waste.

EL ABUSO EN EL CONSUMO DE ESTE PRODUCTO ES NOCIVO PARA LA SALUD

A mi familia.

This novel began as an argument with a friend (and fellow American) that took place in Madrid on June 16, 2007. The plot came to me on a train back to Lisbon. I wrote a rough draft in a cafe called A Brasileira. I went to London, Oporto, and then back to Madrid, where I purchased a copy of Resident Evil 4 for Windows, because I got sick of writing. After arriving in Paris, I spent the days walking the streets. And spent the nights killing zombies. I brought the novel back to my home, Chicago. Then on to New Jersey, New York, Sao Paulo, and Curitiba. On to Mexico City. As we speak, I´m writing this by candle light on a cocktail napkin in Guadalajara. I might be in TJ, tomorrow. Or Las Vegas. I don´t know. Maybe Havana, but I don´t have my Argentine passport with me. So probably not. I want to thank Mike, Andy, and August for dealing with my late hours, and prima donna antics. Andy especially. I pretty much finished the damn thing in his room. My room was too messy. Thanks Andy.

Cheers,

Ernesto "ABSOLUT" Guerrero

Guadalajara, June 2008

An American Fury

Part 1: Childhood in Pieces

It's 106 miles to Chicago, we got a full tank of gas, half a pack of cigarettes, it's dark, and we're wearing sunglasses.

Hit it.

Childhood in Pieces: Actors

Ricardo "Ricky" Alonso Campesino—protagonist

Richard Campesino (father, born in Havana)

Javier Campesino (uncle, born in Havana)

Ricardo Campesino (grandfather, born in Havana)

Teresa Campesino (grandmother of protagonist)

Raquel Campesino (mother of protagonist)

General Ricardo Campesino (born in the Canary Islands, great grandfather to protagonist)

Angela Campesino (born in Naperville, sister of protagonist)

Pedro Facciolo (born in Havana, husband of Lourdes, great uncle to protagonist)

Lourdes Facciolo (sister of Teresa Campesino)

Ruperto Campesino (great uncle of protagonist, lives in Miami)

Eileen Malloy—Highschool love interest of protagonist

an american fury
by
felipe cabrera gutierrez

All knowledge should be used for good
César Chávez

It's 106 miles to Chicago. We've got a full tank of gas, it's dark out, and we're wearing sunglasses.

Hit it.

I met my thesis adviser, and after registering my face, and reading my file, she asked me where I was from. Chicago, I said, not wanting to divulge anything more. She sighed, annoyed at my answer. What's your heritage? She asked. My mother is from Buenos Aires, I confessed, and my father is from Havana. She smiled, pleased that I had elicited the correct response that time. I don't mean this in a negative way, she said, but you look just like— Yeah, I said, interrupting her, you're not the first person to tell me that. During those weeks after the incident, amid the barrage of cameraman and newscasters that had invaded our campus, friends had commented on how similar my features were to the dead man's: about 5'11 in height, olive skin, dark hair, full lips, and dark, brooding eyes. Terrorist's eyes. I had become accustomed to the shocked expressions that confused me with the dearly departed terrorist whose face was splattered all over YouTube, Fox News, and The Times.

I told my thesis adviser that I wanted to write about what happened, and she said that five other people were writing on the same topic, including Mary Reed, the wicked smart, Aderall bottle who was on to track to be the valedictorian. Mary Reed and the others, my thesis adviser said, smugly, bothered to turn in their thesis proposals on time, which you, Mr. Campesino, failed to do. Mary Reed is investigating the event and the terrorist's life from both historical and sociological angles.

I don't give a fuck if her version is better than mine, I said. Mary Reed isn't smart. She's a psycho who gets off on sleep deprivation and calculating her GPA. My thesis adviser looked like she was about to have an aneurysm. Get the hell out of my office, she said. I put my head in my hands, acted like I was having a moment, and squirted a few tears. Ohhh, God, I said. Why am I always so disrespectiful? Why do I always do this? She didn't buy it at first, but told me that she would still discuss it with me if I refrained from cursing and any more misogynistic comments. Thank you from the bottom of my cora-zón, I said. I want to write about my life, about how misunderstood I was as a child, being a person of color. I told her my take on the incident would bring a fresh perspective. A student of color's perspective, and all that jazz. I said I was sorry for my feelings toward Mary Reed. It wasn't my fault. I was a Latino male, stuck in the first act of the core drama of life, reliving the stories of patriarchy and deformation, and strong, intelligent women, like Mary Reed, intimidate me. I need to write about what's happened, I said, not only to understand it, but to explore my own sense of being Latino. My Latino-ness. Her mouth stretched into a lipstick-smeared smile. She ate that shit up like arroz con pollo at an authentic Mexican restaurant. She waved goodbye to me and signed all her subsequent emails with hearts. My Latino-ness gets thesis advisers wet.

I am not a hero. I didn't stop the terrorist. I never served in a war, or worked manual labor because I had to. But hell, I'm smart. I'm really smart. I was smart enough to get into a good college. (Thank you, Affirmative Action)

Ricardo Alonso Campesino
New York, NY, 2008

There were several stains on her comforter. At least five or six wet splotches and one or two tide-pools filled with the residue of my love. These were not the bad kind of stains, the kind that unsuspecting spouses find in the defiled sheets of their wedding beds, the kind that drive these same spouses to their local bar to swallow copious amounts of alcohol, in some hope that they'll be able to forget about their cheating lover. Nor were these stains of the adolescent brand, caused by young boys learning about their bodies. The five or six wet stains, on my girl friend's brand new sun flower yellow comforter, were old. These recently created tide pools, butt-spanking new, looked like a blend of milk and honey, if honey were transparent as opposed to translucent. These last two stains were not induced in the presence of my girlfriend. The other five or six were created earlier, while she was with me. The tide pools I did on my own.

*****

Cities are different things to different people. I found New York beautiful in its grimy way, much grimier than Chicago I knew, and still love. New York was the first time I felt free to be a nerd. Free to express myself. But cities have sinister connotations as well. Corruption can only occur in cities. Diseases thrive in cities. Violence is everywhere. I arrived at Penn Station at seven thirteen that night. My backpack was heavy; within it I had my whole life: my laptop, a couple books, and two pairs of dirty underwear and socks. I had not seen my girl friend in two weeks and our separation from one another had weighed heavily upon my mind. Penn Station smelled like a cross between a men's bathroom and freshly baked pretzels. I waved at a bum who looked about forty, with greasy dread locks. He was a little out of it but was not as depressing as the other bums. I made my way through stunned tourists and disgruntled New Yorkers. I headed down to the 1, slipping through the turnstile, and climbed up the stairs that would take me to the up town. You can see all of God's creatures in the subway.

Before I turned the corner I heard the manic rhythms of a large black man beating a drum kit. He had a picked-out afro and I couldn't help tapping my hand on my thigh as I walked by him. He even had a recorded CD. I thought about donating to him, but I noticed a grandma rocking out on the downtown side and felt embarrassed. I kept tapping my hand on my thigh, but did so *in secret*. I spotted a rat playing in a puddle near the subway track. Despite the fact that I had been coming to New York every other weekend for the last five months, I had never seen a subway rat before. No one believed me, but it was true. I watched the little fellow take a few sips of the not-so-grimy water and go on his way. He wasn't that fat or disgusting. He just looked like a rat. He wasn't bothering anyone.

The 2 pulled in on the other side and I realized it ran express until 96th St. so I, filed in behind a family on vacation. I sat down on the end of the bench and pulled a book out of my bag, the name of which I can't recall because I started to daydream. I hadn't seen my girlfriend, Helen, and I missed her. I really wanted to have sex with her too; it had been a long time. As we started going, a man walked onto our car selling some books. It was called "Bum Poetry" or "Poetry about Bums" or something like that, I can't remember. He had an eye patch and chin-strap facial hair. He handed out a few copies of "Bum Poetry" to some little kids. I thought that was a good idea because the little kids were wearing nice clothes and they would probably ask their parents to buy them a copy of "Bum Poetry". I know I would.

If the time is right, recited the salesman, ain't no need to fight. Girl, together we can last. Let's have some fun and I'll stick it in yo—

LALALALALA, said one of the mothers of those boys holding the fresh copies of "Bum Poetry". She had her hands over her son's ears. I started thinking about my girl friend's bum. I sent her a text message saying that I would be there soon. The message had not gone through, I realized, because I was using my cell phone in an underground tunnel. No one could hear me in there. The message wouldn't go through until I was aboveground, but by then I would already be at Columbia, and Helen wouldn't have known how I had felt about her at that moment when I was underground in the subway car. She wouldn't have known I was thinking about her bum. The train pulled to a stop and I heard the voice announce "*96th Street!*" so I got out of the car, waved goodbye to the kid who owned a new copy of "Bum Poetry" and waited for the next train to arrive. I pictured Helen's face in my mind, her small, shy breasts, and her angular shoulders. Her canary-blonde hair. You could not make up a better woman. I remember the last time we slept together; afterwards, we had spent twenty minutes wrestling and tickling one another. She is much smaller then me; I have about seven inches on her and almost eighty pounds, but she knows how to use her elbows and occasionally wraps her arms and legs around me in such a way that I am unable to move. I can usually get out of it after a few minutes, but she is a powerful bedmate and commands respect.

We pulled into the Columbia stop and I called Helen. I was greeted with an anti-climactic, Hi, this is Helen, I'm not here right now, but—. I hung up and walked up the stairs. I took a left coming out of the turnstile and then took the stairs that went right, which put me right outside Barnard College. You'd think a woman's college would be a great place to go, if you were looking for a woman, because you'd know exactly where to go, which happened to be true in my case, but if you don't have a woman, don't go looking there. Most of them are pretty fugly. Trust me. I slipped in through the side gate that was left open until a certain time of night, and as I walked in I saw Helen standing at the door, waiting for me. Helen Eveline is average height for a girl, but her legs are very long so she looks taller than she is, like a model. She has blonde hair, angular features, and eyes that are yellow in the middle and blue on the outside. We hugged and I kissed her on the head.

I missed yo face, she said before turning to the security guard, giving him her room number and I handed him my school I.D. We made our way to the elevator and I said, I'm going to ravish your body, and she said, We can do that later, but right now we have to go to the Nick Joseph show. My heart sank as I realized I wouldn't be able to spend the next few hours watching movies and drinking orange juice between rounds of getting sticky with my girlfriend.

Do we *have to?* I asked. She nodded and kissed me on the forehead. We walked to her room and I dropped my bag off. She turned to grab her black coat and before she could slip it over her shoulders, I picked her up and carried her to the bed.

Alonso-face, what are you doing? She asked. We have to go to the Nick Joseph show. I'm not having sex with you. But then I did my secret sexy move and I put her down and I lay down on the bed. Then I wrapped my legs around her and pulled her close to me and we started making out hardcore and in my head, I was like, Yeeeaaaaaah. Then she did that evil thing that girls can do and she pulled back and said, I love you, but we can't have sex right now. We promised Rachael last week that we'd go to the Nick Joseph show. And in my head I was like, No, Helen, no! Screw the show. Let's stay here and *make love*. But she was being all crazy like girls can be and not wanting to *make love*, so I put my coat back on and made a pouty face. We went back downstairs and then down to the subway. I couldn't stop thinking about making love and the feeling of her nose brushing against mine and the rocking of her hips. Her hot breath and sweat between our stomachs. The look on her face made me wanna—

I came back to my senses. She looked at me and said, What? smiling just as she pronounced the "t". I get a chill whenever she does it; it's cute. I said, Nothing, baby. I was just thinking about yo bum. She made a squirrel face at me then stuck her tongue out. I ignored her, so she licked my face. The woman next to us scooted away. I licked her cheek.

We have to stop doing this in public.

I blame you, I said. A weird couple walked into the car and Helen whispered into my ear, *Why don't you have green hair?*

I can dye it if you want. I can dye yours, too, so we'll match.

Only if you let me tickle your balls in public.

We arrived at the show and said hello to all of our friends, which was fine, but I just wanted to get out of there so we could get back to Helen's room like it was rush hour, and *get down to business, if you know what I mean.* Our friend Nick Joseph stepped on stage and began playing his John Mayer-esque love odes and the ladies in the crowd started to rock their hips back and forth and the cool dudes at the bar with the flat-brim hats were 24-chillin' with some Coronas because they had fake ID's, but I didn't have one so I was sitting next to my girlfriend on a couch, while she was talking to other girls, about stuff, but I still nodded my head at those dudes and I was like, *Yeah. I'm just as cool as you, even if I don't have a fake to buy over-rated beer with.* I kept making these sexy faces at Helen, and she giggled, because I was so funny, and but then she would just walk away. I don't think she understand that I really wanted to have sex with her at that moment. Nick Joseph finished up with his last song, called "Hot Shot" and I remember this smooth lyric he said really fast: *Picture, picture, picture, photograph/ Is worth—four thousand words.* I couldn't get the lyric out of my head for the rest of the night and neither could Helen so the entire subway ride back, Helen and I kept singing to one another and making out like crazy, because we were getting ready for all the crazy sex we were going to have once we got back to her apartment. We pulled into the stop at 116th and I jumped out of the long train car, pulling Helen with me. She was laughing, and we ran all the way to her door, but I beat her there. She checked me into the wall, and ran ahead, so I ran her down and stuck my tongue in her mouth, which she hates. We were playing tonsil hockey. She pushed me into the wall again and ran down to her room. I went to the bathroom and when I entered her room, she was under the cover in panties and this sexy gray v-neck she always wears. I jumped in bed, ready to play some more tonsil hockey, and make love, but then she looked at me with her bottom lip sticking out and said, Baby, I'm tired. I've got sorority initiations tomorrow. Can we just go to bed? And then my penis fell off. Now I know what you're thinking. You're thinking, Barnard College doesn't officially recognize sororities; this Ricky guy is full of shit. Well let me tell you, that just because a university doesn't recognize Greek organizations, that doesn't mean they don't exist, or enact a certain amount of influence on social events. If any of you readers are interested in attending Barnard College, remember that, and tell your lady friends, because they don't put that in the brochure. You can tell them that Ricky told you.

I put on my good boyfriend face and I was like, Yeah, baby it's cool. We don't have to have sex, let's brush our teeth, and cuddle and fall asleep in one another's arms. She smiled at me and I was like, Yeah, I know what that means. So we brushed our teeth and just as we were about to go to bed, I spooned her and…

*Well, hello ther*e Benicio… She said. My penis may or may not be named after Benicio del Toro. My heart started beating really fast because I knew that she liked it and then she turned to me and said.

I love you, Ricky-face, but let's go to sleep. She kissed me and then fell asleep in my arms and I was disappointed for about ten minutes, but then I felt really good because she was there with me in my arms, but just about when I realized that, I fell asleep. I must have had some crazy sex dreams, because when I woke up, Benicio was excited. The sunshine was creeping in, but I looked around and Helen wasn't there. I was still tired so I went back to sleep. When I woke up again, I checked the clock and it was two in the afternoon. Suddenly Helen walked in, back from sorority initiations. She was all sweaty and beautiful and I gave her my sexy look and she was like, Yeah, Ricky, oh yeah. We started making out and then her clothes melted off and we started having all this crazy sex. The bed was jumping and everyone was yelling and we were saying stuff to each other that we would never say to anyone else. That went on for so long that I don't even remember, and then we cuddled. She got up and went to the bathroom. I got excited because I was so happy about where I was that I got a boner again. I started thinking about her and then next thing I know I was standing over the bed and coming all over her new sheets. That's when I noticed the stains all over the place and the brand new tide pools I had just created. I sat there for a second and marveled at my creation, but at this point, Helen returned from the bathroom, looking all fresh and beautiful like she always does, but I still had my hand on my penis.

Ricky! She said, what are you doing? Oh my god, did you just jerk off? On to the bed? Your seed is all over my sheets! She started laughing and hitting my back and I said, No, no, stop hitting me. Please, stop. She wouldn't stop laughing until, finally, she said, Ricky, you could have waited for me to come back, or at least jerked off *into a piece of paper*. Not on my brand new yellow sheets! Why did you *do that*? She said the last part in a cute voice. I gave her my sexy look, and then I said, real serious-like, 'Cus I love you, baby.

I had my own room in my grandparents' house on Green Street. Hidden between the television room and the living room, behind an oak door with a paper grocery bag taped to it, warning intruders in misspelled crayon. There was a bed and a window, which connected the wall of my room with a wall in the living room. I asked my grandfather, who was in the living room, why it was there.

Un niño enfermo vivía aquí. Creo que la madre lo miraba por la ventana. My heart went mushy when I thought of a sick, little boy, sleeping in my room. I wanted to ask my grandfather another question, but he had disappeared from my field of vision. I looked through the window, at the green couch with rose patterns, my grandfather's recliner, the old wooden television set, and out the window at Green Street, and little kids across the street, like I imagined the sick boy used to. I spied my mother, inspecting her new tennis outfit in the mirror. She pushed aside strands of hair to frame her face, and pouted her lips in the mirror like a cover girl. Blonde streaks cut through the rest of her hair, which was dark like mine. I inspected her face. She looked just like me.

Mommy, why did you dye your hair? I called through the open window.

Because you told me I look ugly with dark hair, she said, smirking.

When did I say that? I said. She ran her fingers through her hair as she walked over to me, and then pushed the window a little farther down.

When you were a baby, she said. Her kiss was soft and warm, tickling my forehead like a bird's feather. Be good, she called, as she closed the door behind her. She played tennis five days a week. My grandmother was in the kitchen cooking lunch. I could hear her parakeet, Michaelangelo, chirping over the sound of butter frying in a pan.

Michaelangelo was named after my favorite Ninja Turtle, whose action figure I held in my eager hand. I climbed through the window, looked out the window at the kids playing soccer across the street, and decided to watch television.

When I was very young, I watched hours and hours of television. Nickelodeon, mostly. Salute Your Shorts and Wild and Crazy Kids were my favorite shows. Teenage Mutant Ninja Turtles. I had a crush on the brown-haired girl from Hey, Dude, a show about kids on a ranch. Are you Afraid of the Dark? was scary, but not too scary. I watched kid shows, too. Gullah Gullah Island. Blue's Clues. Arthur. Get Smart was my favorite show on Nick at Night. I loved Agent Smart. I had a crush on Penny. I could stand Bewitched, but I liked the first Darrin a lot more than the second Darrin. I had a crush on Samantha. I watched a lot of cartoons: Doug, Rocko's Modern Life, Looney Toons, Tiny Toons. I watched I Love Lucy, of course. I had seen every episode, and some other movies that Lucille Ball had starred in. Even though I knew I was named after my father (who had changed his name to Richard before I was born), and his father, I liked to imagine that I was named after Ricky Ricardo. Even though my grandmother was Cuban, she had curly hair like Lucille Ball, so I used to imagine she was my grandmother and Ricky Ricardo was my grandfather. Little ricky was my dad. I thought the TV show was about them, even though I knew my dad grew up poor. For a while, that made sense, but then I thought about how my family was and changed my schema. Lucy and Ricky got rich, like my dad and my mom were. So my dad, Richard, was Ricky Ricardo, even though my dad spoke English with no accent, because he had grown up in Naperville like me. My mom, Raquel, was Lucy, which still didn't fit, because Lucy had curly hair and spoke English perfectly. My mom had straight hair, and spoke English with a funny accent, because she was from Argentina. According to that schema, I was the real Little Ricky. I didn't figure all that out until I had seen all six seasons. I was seven at the time. I was curious about the actors of these shows and my grandma never hesitated to give me juicy details.

What happened to the first Darrin from Bewitched, grandma?

I donno. The second Darrin was a homosexual. She pronounced it *homosecksual.*

What's that?

He like to have sexual relation with men, she said, as she sprinkled onions into the frying pan. They touch each other penis. My grandmother was a nurse and liked to use medical terms around me, like penis, instead of the more colloquial, pee pee. I didn't ask any more questions about second Darrin.

What were Lucy and Ricky like in real life? Did you ever meet them?

No, I never meet them. They were marry and have children and were very happy, then they divorce. Ricky's real name was Desi Arnaz. He have problem with alcohol and die.

What about Lucy?

She was very successful, but she die too. She pronounced it *sooksesful*.

*****

During the last month of school, the kindergarteners always put on a production of the stations of the Cross. There were actors and readers. Actors played out th actions of the various characters, but were not allowed to speak. The readers read from small white booklets made of computer paper, narrating the play, and speaking for the actors. The readers were often the smarter kids in the class. Mrs. Wozniak, my teacher, announced the selections for the different parts. She announced the readers first. I didn't make the cut.

Maggie Wimpo will be Veronica. Jerry, John, and Marco will be Guards #1,2,and 3. Tyler will be Pontius Pilate. Freddie will be Joseph, the apostle. Harry S. will be Peter. Harry R. will be Judas--

Harry's a Judas! Harry's a Judas!

Derek, be quiet or you'll be receiving *two* sad news notes this week. Gregory will be Thomas... Nancy will be Mary. I think that's it. I felt like an idiot. I was so terrible a student that I wasn't even allowed in the kindergarten play. Maybe they would send me back to preschool. Hopefully not the one in Argentina. I had trouble speaking Spanish and all the other kids had called me *gringo*. Maybe Mrs. Wozniak would let me be an usher.

Mrs. Wozniak?

Yes, Maggie.

Who's gonna be Jesus?

Oh, right. Ricky will be playing Jesus.

Crucify Ricky! Crucify Ricky!

When I was still in my infant years, I used to ask my grandmother to tell me stories about her life in the white house near the ocean. Before the men with the guns came down from the mountains.

On the weekends we used to sit in the living room together in the old house on Green Street. My father put her in bad moods when he came home from work.

Este hijo mío. Es insoportable. She said, referring to my father. ¿Algún de tus amigos necesita una criada? Limpio. Lavo la ropa. Cuido a los niños. Necesito un rinconcito. Nada mas.

Funny, grandma. What's a rinconcito?

A corner for me to sleep in, she said. I was the only person who could get my grandmother to rest for a minute, between taking care of the rose garden, the laundry, and other responsilities she had in the house on Green St. where she lived with my grandfather. We lived a few minutes a way, but we always ate dinner there, and I often stayed there when my mother had tennis lessons. There were always distractions, but I paid them no attention, my eyes were focused on her steel-rimmed glasses and her curly blonde-tinted hair. I called her grandma. Her given name was Teresa Campesino. She addressed me like this: *mi cielo. My sky. My heaven.*

She had been an amateur painter in Cuba, as well as a teacher, but I was her only student then, attending lectures on how to treat girls when on a date or how to sketch cardinals. My favorite subject was history, specifically the history of my grandparents' lives, which began in Havana, and continued in what was once a small farm town outside Chicago: Naperville, IL. The watershed year, at least in our history, was 1959, when Castro and the rest of the Barbudos came down from the Sierra Maestra to take control of the country. The protagonists of the stories, my grand-father, his father, and my father, who were all at one time named Ricardo, spent the rest of their lives dealing with the fallout of the Revolution.

Despite her strong accent, my grandmother was a wonderful storyteller; she slipped from English to Spanish as a rainbow moves from blue to red. All the while, my grandfather was in the garage, working in a haze of sharp screeches, sawdust, and sweat, meticulously crafting every piece of furniture in my room. Twenty years after leaving Havana, and his white-collared job as a lawyer, my grandfather discovered that he had a love for carpentry.

During the weekdays I stayed at my grandparents' house, like my sister would do after me. My father took me to school during the mornings and my mother or my grandparents picked me up. I liked it when my grandparents picked me up. My grandfather wore a ratty, gray fedora atop his silver head, and a red and black flannel shirt. He had a jet black mustache and squirrelly eyebrows, divided by a pair of Yon Lenín glasses. The color of his mustache wasn't real; he had dyed it after seeing a Just For Men commercial with Rafi Palmeiro. Everyone said he looked ridiculous, but I said he looked good. After all, he had made all the furniture in my room.

My grandmother wore black earmuffs that day. She smiled and hugged my head.

My mother was another thing entirely. She was usually late to pick me up from school. I used to hang out with this blonde kid named Whitey and play wall ball after the parking lot was empty. His mother was often late, too. Once when I was in kindergarten, my mother brought me to school on a day when the kindergartener's were off, and a third-grader named Amrit had to take me to the principal's office, where I waited an hour for her to come pick me up. I was angry with her that day. My mother embarrassed me because she spoke with an accent; she is from Argentina and never learned to speak English as well as my father. He had no accent because he grew up in Illinois like me. She moved to Illinois when she had me.

I was proud of my mother, though. She was glamorous, much more so than other mothers of Sts. Peter and Paul Elementary School. She was very beautiful, and Argentine, and could read and write in three languages. She had freckled, olive skin, deep brown eyes, and dark hair. Her clothes were colorful and her purses were made by Louis Vuitton and Coach. She played tennis at the country clubs in Naperville and she used to brag to me about how she beat some of the other mothers. One thing she did, which annoyed me very much, was hug me too tight. One time at recess, a group of us were having a discussion over who had the prettiest mother. Most of the other boys conceded, but one boy named Geoffrey continued to argue with me until Mrs. Taylor told us to quit yapping during multiplication tables. Geoffrey and I never came to an agreement, but I think he knew who was right.

*****

I did not enjoy sports when I was young. They used to let us out twice a day for recess and I would wander around the blacktop with my friends Peter and Jeff. The other boys played football in the street, but it never made much sense to me. It just looked like they chased a ball around and stopped intermittently. I didn't learn what a "down" was until eighth grade. I used to categorize everything in my head: I called the ball-chasers "jocks", Jeff, Peter, and I were "funnies" because we were drawn to the more interesting things in life. Jokes, conversation, and girls. We were advanced for second graders, sporting blue oxfords, navy blue khakis, and bowl cuts, except for Jeff, who had a buzz. We wandered around the blacktop, telling jokes, occasionally stealing the ball from the "jocks" and throwing it in a random direction, and sometimes talking to girls. The first time I spoke with Leja was on the blacktop.

Once this philistine named Mark pegged me in the face with the football because he was mad that I had thrown it across the street. Peter and I had stolen it from the group of boys. My nose stung, but I didn't retaliate. He called me a faggot, but I had no idea what that meant.

*****

Grandma! Grandpa! I said.

Ricky, we miss you today! How was school? She said and hugged me.

Hola, mi nieto, My grandfather said, Vámonos. Tengo un regalo para ti en casa.

Really? What is it? Tell me! Tell me! I said.

You see at home, my grandmother said, and we got into the old Camry and left the parking lot.

Sts. Peter and Paul Elementary School was located near the downtown which we had to drive through in order to get home.

Este town. Todo ha cambiado aquí.

Sí, my grandmother said. When they first moved here, in 1965, Naperville had been a little farming community outside Chicago where everyone knew one another. There were a few stores in the downtown; Oswald's pharmacy was still there. There was a bowling alley where the Barnes and Noble stood. The block with the Ralph Lauren Store, the Coach Store, and The Sharper Image used to be a parking lot for the grocery.

We pulled up to my grandparent's home on Green Street. My grandfather parked the car outside of the garage.

"Vén, Ricky." My grandfather said. My grandmother took my backpack inside and we went into the garage. There were unpainted chests and chairs, scattered pieces of wood, and the scent of sawdust in the air. My grandfather looked around inquisitively, as if he was asking the garage where something was. He pulled some boxes down from a shelf and rummaged through them. I stared at the line of handsaws hanging from the wall. Long, serrated gashes of metal. He grew impatient and started digging through the countertops littered with stiff bits of material and strings. He stopped and opened up a drawer. He pulled out a little wooden pipe he had made and handed to me.

"Oh yay!" I said, "Thank you, grandpa." He nodded. I had asked him to make it for me a few weeks earlier. I wanted a pipe ever since I first saw my idol on television, Popeye the sailor man. I hated spinach, but thanks to my grandfather, I had a pipe just like him. I was still too young to smoke but I imagined little red embers in the bowl, releasing tufts of blue smoke, spreading through the air. My lacquered one of the oak chests which lay on his counter; he always used the same stain. I asked why he never painted them interesting colors—bright blue or red like strawberries. He said he liked the stain because it brought out the natural essence of the wood. My father agreed with him when I asked his opinion. I thought they looked nice but I always thought he could have made them so much more interesting. I often sat in the garage and watched my grandfather work, but I failed to learn very much from him. I built a bird house once for Boy Scouts; I think my parents still have it. Sometimes my grandfather would give me a few pieces of wood and a hammer, but as soon as he would give them to me, my imagination went bare. I would take two pieces of wood, arrange them perpendicular to one another and strike the head of the nail, but it never turned out right. A nail was always sticking out and I never seemed to reap anything worthy of all the time I had sacrificed. Crooked crosses were the only thing I was good at making. Despite all the time I spent in that garage I never learned to use the electric saw.

The stand was heavy and painted black. It frightened me. My grandfather told me I would never make anything of value if I did not learn to use the saw. Whenever he used it, I covered my hands with my ears. I hated the saw. I used to take shelter in front of the television with my grandmother. She treated me like a prince. She let me sit in my grandfather's recliner and watch whatever I liked.

Tengas hijos. She said to me once. Para cuando estés viejo, pueden ayudarte.

OK, grandma.

Among a variety of things she made my favorites: fried skirt steak, black beans with rice, fried sweet plantains, and hash browns. Afterwards, she usually served strawberry ice cream, my grandfather's favorite. The things she made for me were always a jumble of American and Cuban cuisine. They didn't sell the right kind of food at Jewel so we would drive to the Mexican grocery in Aurora. We bought my favorite crackers—large flat galletas with guayabada spread on them. I went with her to that Mexican grocery a few times, but I was frightened because people said that Aurora was a bad place, that there were gangs there. I never saw any gangs at that market.

*****

Do you know who the greatest hero in Cuban history is?

Ricky Ricardo?

No seas bobo. Have you ever heard of José Martí?

I think so.

José Martí was the greatest Cuban patriot. He spent his life in exile in New York City, writing and campaigning for democracy in Cuba. He was also a poet.

Do you know any of his poetry?

Cultivo una rosa Blanca

en junio como en enero
para el amigo sincero
que me da su mano franca.

Y para el cruel que me arranca
el corazón con que vivo,
cardo ni ortiga cultivo;
cultivo la rosa blanca.

That's very pretty, grandma. You sing nice.

Thank you. I learn it in school when I was a little girl. My teacher used to slap me on my hand. She say I don't sing well. She was a bad teacher. She was very mean to me.

How did José Martí die?

He died at la Batalla de Dos Rios, fighting for Cuba. He was a hero.

Did Fidel kill him?

No, Fidel came later. Fidel took over when Batista was there. Batista was bad as well.

If Fidel beat a bad man, then doesn't that make him good?

We think that in the beginning, but no, unfortunately that is not the case.

Grandma, if Fidel is bad, why did he win? George Washington and Abraham Lincoln won. They're good; that's why the United State won.

Because the good people don't always win, Ricky. Every place isn't like the United State.

So we lost... And we're here now?

Yes. You need to know, Ricky, that no place is perfect. Cuba was not perfect. Even though the U.S. give us a chance to be free, it have its' problem, too. They treat the black people very terrible here. You know, when I was in Cuba, we did not have race problem like here. The black people were poor but it was not like here. But I don't like to criticize the United State, because when we left Cuba, President Eisenhower gave us money and a place to live. Spain didn't want us, even though my mother was from Barcelona and your grandfather's father was from the islands. England didn't want us either. The United State was the one. The United State give us a chance, for that I will always be grateful.

Oh.

*****

When I used to teach in Cuba, I bring some of the student to my house. I gave them galletas and coffee. Habia una negrita que era mi favorita. Era una buena chiquita. Rezaba mucho para ella.

Why didn't their parents do that? Why did you pray for the girl?

Because they weren't around or they didn't have the money. Because there were bad men who did a very bad thing to her.

If I was president, I would give a million dollars to everyone. What did they do to her?

It's not that simple, Ricky.

Why not?

Porque la vida es dura.

That's stupid. I'm glad it's not like that here.

It is like that here. Not everyone is as lucky as we are.

No, it can't be. The U.S. is good.

*****

My grandfather loved to talk about the movies.

When I go to the movie in Cuba, for ten cent I get to see two full movies and a cartoon. Also, a Coke for your grandma and me, and a tin of goiabada and crackers. All this for only ten cent! His eyes lit up and he said this. He smelled of cologne from Sears.

*****

One night my grandmother made flan, my grandfather's favorite dessert. I didn't like it and refused to finish it, which angered my grandfather. He responded by saying that I watched too much television. They talked about me in Spanish, right in front of me, thinking I couldn't understand. My grandfather began to shout. I might not have been able to respond, but I understood every word, so I left the kitchen and went upstairs to my room. When my grandmother came up to comfort me, she told me a story about the first time she saw the Andes. She had been in her twenties.

Grandpa: Are you gettin any? You can tell me. Are you gettin' any?
Dwayne: [*shakes his head no*]
Grandpa: Christ! What are you? 15? My God man! You gotta be gettin' that young stuff! The young stuff is the best stuff in the world. Your jail bait, they're jail bait. You turn sixteen and you're looking at three to five.

-Little Miss Sunshine

Warmth. A twinge of wetness, hot at the touch, then a cold, comfortable tingling.

At the opening of my dream it felt like someone was kissing me. I could never really be sure, because in the morning I could only remember the sensation on my cheek. Shades of feeling lingered: a warmth or a chill running down my chest and lower, like a rivulet of liquid. It could have been my mother sneaking into my room after I fell asleep. Her quick steps. Her thin cotton nightgown with the indistinguishable flowers. Her repeated affections, her small shoulders, and her vice-like grip. Her sloppy kisses. I love you, I love you, I love you.

Or it could have been my father. Musky t-shirt and boxers. Wide, round shoulders. Big stomach. The thick brush of his mustache on my cheek. Bald head, and home from work. One kiss was plenty. I love you, son. My cheeks stung afterwards.

It could have been my grandmother. Her slow deliberate step. Her thin wrists and tired hands held close to her body. Her beige bathrobe. The funny way she looked without her glasses. Opening a vat of Vicks Vap-O-Rub (being hit hard by the smell), slipping her greasy, scented hand beneath the lip of my shirt, and dabbing the mint salve on my chest, tickling me, into hysterical laughter, asking me to stop laughing so she could go to bed. One kiss from her. Te quiero, mi cielo. She left the door a little bit open. I was still giggling when she left.

*****

My father shook me awake. My vision was fuzzy and the light stung my eyes like water. Why did I have to go to school?

Dad, ten minutes.

No. You're getting up now.

DAD, TEN MINUTES.

OK. Jesus.

It had taken me some time to fall asleep the night before, and I could feel it in my limbs and my back. My thighs were sore from basketball practice. Too much running, up and down the court. Up and down the court. Ten minutes was just enough to fall asleep *again.* I could see the curve of—

Ricky, wake up, my father said. It's been ten minutes. He wore a suit.

Uuunhhhhh, I moaned, like a lion cub.

Ricky, I'm not going through this with you again. Get your butt out of bed. My father ripped the comforter off my body and the air felt like ice water. Curled into the fetal position, I wore nothing but whitey-tighties and a Ninja Turtles t-shirt. I slowly slid my legs off the edge of the bed, and toddled to the dresser where I had my socks, underwear, and a black Sony stereo that had belonged to my father. My first three albums were: Chumbawumba's *Tubthumping*, Coolio's *Gangsta's Paradise*, and the Beatles' *Please Please Me*. My father had confiscated Chumbawumba because they said *pissing the night away* in the song, *I get knocked down, but I get up again. You're never gonna keep me down.* I had felt that this "violation of my property rights was both unwarranted and egregious", but he just told me to get a job. My father had not confiscated Coolio yet, despite track nine's clever title, *Fucc Coolio.* I slid *Please Please Me* into the slot and within a few seconds, between whirrs and zips, Paul was singing. *Well she was just 17, if you know what I me-an. And the way she looked, was way beyond compare...*

Ejaculations of middle school expression colored the once-white walls of my room.

I had cut out pictures of full-grown women, like Britney Spears, Jennifer Lopez, and Angelina Jolie, emphasizing the curves of their hips and their breasts. And Angelina's lips. I slept beneath the full-formed glory of my seductresses, but the highest reaches of my room were filled with posters of gods and rocks stars. Dr. Dre. Nirvana. Green Day. Sublime. Rage against the Machine. The Red Hot Chili Peppers. As I looped my new black belt through my pair of plain navy khakis, I rocked out to *Suck My Kiss*.

Well I'm sa-i-ling... The bass pounded. The posters waved and scraped the walls, and the trinkets and quarters on my wardrobe clinked together. I jumped on my bed, strumming with my right hand and whipping my head violently. *Hit me you cant hurt me.* Suck my kiss. *Kiss me please pervert me.* Stick with this. *Is she talking dirt-ee? Give to me sweet sacred bliss; your mouth was made to* suck my kiss...

I slipped my pants on, and grabbed one of the many light blue oxfords in my closet. They were all long-sleeved, and looked awkward when I didn't roll the sleeves, but they were much better than the short-sleeved shirts, which made me look like a kindergartner. I turned off the stereo, cutting the Beatles off midline, and rushed downstairs.

The kitchen was regular, with white tiles, beige walls, and a ripe, green vine painted above the doorway. The Dow was skyrocketing that day, and Jordan had scored thirty in the fourth the night before. The Cinnamon Toast Crunch tasted delicious, which made me feel optimistic about the day. I drank the sweet fake cinnamon milk left in the bottom of the bowl.

I brushed my teeth and investigated myself in the mirror. I was a tall boy with long forearms and a confusion of black hair. My arms looked too skinny, like girl's arms. I had a trickle of hair on my chest, but I was waiting for my muscles to show up. My dad called me and I ran downstairs. I put on my big puffy coat and laced my black Dock Martens.

My mother had given me hell for wanting black shoes instead of brown ones, which most other boys had.

I like the black ones, I had said.

No, she said. All your friends have brown shoes. They will make fun of you.

I don't care. I want the black ones. Why can't I have the black ones?

Ricky, do you want to have friends?

What does that have to do with anything?

Ricky, if you wear black shoes, you won't have any friends. Nobody wears black shoes. Everybody wears brown shoes.

Mom, if you don't buy me these shoes I'm not going to school anymore. She bought me the black belt to match the shoes. I was no longer her doll to play dress up with.

I tried to sleep during the fifteen minute ride to school, but the traffic was heavy and I was worried I would be late. We listened to National Public Radio.

I didn't hate school, but it was just so boring. It seemed that the teachers did everything they could to make learning as slow and uneventful as possible. Mrs. Carpshaw wrote out pre-algebra problems on the green chalkboard with pasty chalk. Once I was chosen to write the answer on the board, but I got the wrong answer, because I hadn't been paying attention. I felt embarrassed for the rest of the day and smelled like chalk from clapping the erasers together. In social studies, we sat and read from a text book. If you were good at reading, you got bored, because reading out loud took too long, and if you were bad at reading, you were embarrassed because you sounded like a retard.

My friend Peter was sick so I had no one to talk to. In history class they were learning about Columbus. It seemed like the only thing they ever did in history class was learn about Columbus. The teacher would have them take turns out of the text book with the big print, which they all had in front of them on the desk. *The Columbian Exchange. Potatoes, horses, and syphilis.* I had never heard of a fruit or animal called syphilis.

Math class was almost as boring as history. They were doing something called pre-algebra, which consisted of multiplication and division problems with a question mark inserted for one of the numbers. For one of the problems, the teacher wrote 3*? = 33. The math teacher insisted that they use an asterisk in place of an x for the multiplication symbol. never understood her deluded reasoning for doing so, nor had he any desire to. The teacher asked the class if they knew how to solve the problem. The annoying girl with the eager look in her eye raised her hand. Ricky knew the answer but kept his mouth shut and hand down. The teacher called on a boy named Lenny, who opened his mouth and said *uhhhhhhhhhh*. The teacher called on someone else. Lenny had big eyes and whenever you said anything to him he stared at you as if you had just disproved gravity.

Lunch was my favorite part of the day because I got to hang out with my friends and I got to see Leja (rhymes with *playa*) Valenta, who was, in my opinion, the most beautiful girl in the fifth grade. I was in Mrs. Gotko's class and Leah was in Mrs. Scarpino's.

I had spoken with Leja only a few times in the six years that we had been in school together. From what I could gather, she was part Czech, and had an affinity for the Spice Girls. She had long dirty blonde hair and full, tanned legs. Her breasts were beginning to show beneath her yellow blouse, and she had the most exquisite pair of lips I had ever seen. They were a lightish shade of pink, thin yet spilling over. Leja made my heart beat all the more heavily.

I searched the lunch room, walking back and forth, but I never found her. The group of girls that she hung out with had sneaked off to the bathroom. I sat down at my illustrious table, full of jocks. I didn't particularly like sports, neither did Peter or Jeff, but we sat with them because we thought they were cool, and they thought we were funny. My chubby friend, Connor, began reciting some rap song with lots of weird words for different body parts while my other friends, guys like Morice and Stockus, banged on the table to keep rhythm. Despite his fondness for Pop Tarts, Fruit Roll Ups, and other types of treats, Jeff was physically powerful and athletically gifted. He was the only kid in the fifth grade who could hit the softball out of the parking lot. His father had played football for Michigan and the New York Giants, running a 4.75 forty, *as a lineman.* I pounded the table with my left hand and slipped chips into my mouth with the other. My mom had packed me a ham sandwich on white bread, but it was gross from sitting too long.

Connor cleared his throat, and spoke: *Slob* on my *knob*, like *corn* on the *cob*. Check in with me, and do your job. Lay on the bed, and give me head. Don't have to ask, don't have to beg. Juicy is my name, sex is my game. Let's call the boys, let's run a train. Squeeze on my nuts, lick on my butt.

Last call for paper towels, kids, said Mrs. Doolin over the PA. We ignored her and kept banging on the table.

Hit it from the back, Connor continued. Enjoy the sound. Lay on the cover, always use the rubber. Till I got caught, fucking with her mother. She blamed it on me, we fought in the street. She pulled out a knife, so I had to flee. Called up the boys, went to her house. Charged the whole place, threw the bitch out. Police busted in, where the niggas at. We left just in time, and never came back. Roll through the hood, waving at the freaks. Who's sniffing all the rocks, and smoking all the geeks.

Is anybody listening to me? Mrs. Doolin asked over the PA.

That's a funny ass song, Morice said.

That song is retarded, Peter said, laughing.

What the fuck are you talking about? Connor said, with a toothy smile. That song is great. Peter shook his head. I finished my chocolate milk and tossed into the garbage can.

What are you doing? Mr. Port said.

Throwing my lunch away.

You know very well you're supposed to throw out your garbage at a specified time. Sit down. I walked back to my table, but just as I did, Mrs. Doolin called for us to throw away our garbage and move upstairs to the gym.

Stupid Mr. Port, I said under my breath.

We filed into the gym. The junior high kids were already there.

Something big must be going on, I thought. My friends and I kept formation as we moved into the bleachers, making sure to look nonchalant in front of the older kids. We sat down and looked around. There were so many kids, how could the teachers keep control of all of us together like this? I wondered. A third grader with A.D.D. began screaming and jumping. Mrs. Gleason, one of the junior high teachers, escorted him out of the gym.

He pissed his pants, someone said, laughing.

Leja and her friends filed in front of us. I tried to make eye contact with her but she turned her head away quickly. I thought of saying hi to one of her friends but, thought it best not to. My friends ignored the girls.

The principal, Mr. Delvin, went behind the podium and began to speak. My eyes were stuck to the back of Leja's head like a wet tongue to a frozen flagpole. Leja's friends giggled and one of them pushed her shoulder. Leja turned around and looked at me, then looked away quickly. I turned to my friend Steve.

Dude, what's going on?

Katie just kissed Morice.

Huh? Are they boyfriend and girlfriend?

No. *This is weird.*

Mr. Delvin continued to speak, but no one was listening. I leaned in to hear what my friends were saying, but I was the man on the end, so I couldn't get any closer, because everyone was leaning away from me. I turned back to find Leja looking straight at me. Her lips were parted in a coquettish smirk and the top two buttons of her blouse were unbuttoned; I could see the smooth, curved skin above her frilled, pink bra. She stood up and kissed me hard on the mouth. Her lips were soft and wet with cherry lip gloss. Her neck and hair smelled like flowers and Victoria's Secret. My chest felt warm and I parted my lips, moving my tongue to the opening of my mouth. My grip tightened on my knee, and suddenly my penis became hard. She pulled her head back, and I felt a sinking feeling in my chest as I realized my vulnerability. Everyone around us had just witnessed my first kiss. Her friends enveloped her back into their fold, giggling wildly. I stared at the back of her head, my mouth still open, and my head spinning in a mixture of ecstasy and bemusement. I cracked a wide, toothy grin and took deep breaths, in and out, in and out. Endorphins continued to whiz through my brain, as my shirt and pants seemed to tighten around my body. One of my friends tried to give me a high five, but I just smiled and adjusted my belt.

At the end of the assembly, Leja ran to the bathroom followed by her troop. One of the girls stayed behind and approached me. She was the mean one who looked like a dinosaur.

The only reason Leja kissed you, she said, was because she lost an Oreo twist, so take that stupid smile off your face. She's in the bathroom right now washing her mouth out ‘cus you’re so gross. I opened my mouth to call her a bitch but she sped away. I felt a twinge of pain in my chest, and my eyes were hot and wet.

I was a country school-teacher then, fresh from the East, and had never seen a Southern Negro revival…

Those who have not thus witnessed the frenzy of a Negro revival in the untouched backwoods of the South can but dimly realize the religious feeling of the slave; as described, such scenes appear grotesque and funny, but as seen they are awful.

—Chapter X: Of the Faith of Our fathers, The Souls of Black Folks, W.E.B. DuBois

My grandparents received a white, embroidered wedding invitation from their niece, Mirta, who lived in Miami. We had known of the wedding for some time, but it was not until the invitation arrived that my family addressed the issue of who would attend. My father could not go because of work obligations. My mother had never been to Miami and had not seen the Miami relatives since her wedding.

¿Miami? Creo que no, she said. Prefiero Paris. She wouldn't go.

My grandparents were both happy to go; my grandmother loved weddings and my grandfather had not seen his brothers in two years. One of them, Federico, had skin cancer and had just begun his chemo sessions. It was decided that I would attend the wedding, also. I had never been to Miami before, and if anything, they thought it would help me with my Spanish. I had never traveled anywhere, other to school or the 7-11, with my grandparents. We arrived at the airport only two hours before our flight and my grandfather allowed me to hold my airline ticket, which my father never did. I spent the flight watching a movie called *The Birdcage*, which was about a gay couple whose son marries a woman. I didn't understand what *gay* was, so I found the idea of a couple with one man dressed in drag quite ridiculous. I thought it was funny at first, but there were sexual overtones, which made me uncomfortable, because I couldn't understand them.

We arrived in Miami on a Sunday evening. A short, wide-hipped woman with large breasts greeted me at the gate.

Hola, Ricky. Dame un besito. ¿Me recuerdas? Soy tu Tía Juanita. She squeezed my back, holding me longer than I would have liked. I nodded dumbly, unable to answer in Spanish. Her husband, my uncle Ruperto, appeared in the bathroom door and walked towards us. He had a round stomach and slicked back hair.

Este niño ha crecido mucho, ¿no? He said, stepping forward with self-confidence. I nodded my head and smiled. He pointed at me and asked ¿Este niño habla español?

My grandmother winked at me and said that I was quite able.

Sí, I said, feeling dumb and alienated.

Pues, my uncle Ruperto said, verás, sobrino, que Miami es muy distinto de Chee-cago. Hablámo cubano aquí.

*****

Las cuerdas sonan... It was a rare foggy Miami evening and the women spoke Spanish. The colors on the buildings were neon and worn through the open window of Tío Ruperto's restored 1956 Chevy BelAir, a two-door hardtop with a white and green paintjob and leather interior. I stuck my head out the window and checked the reflection in the mirror, lights flashed over the bright yellow awning of a Cuban restaurant, nothing else discernible in the mist. *Son de Negros en Oriente* played on the vintage radio. The DJ's voice was deep and booming with a rhythmic cadence: *Coca tá tocando en los timbales. ¡Ven! el ritmo te llama. Tenémo Manuel el Guajiro tocando en la trompeta y lo hermano Cabrera en los Tres. ¡Sus dedos mueven como arañitas! Y para todo lo americano, my name ees Gallego. I wan to welcome jew to Mee-ami oon dis wonderful, fuggy ev-uning. Ees a rare teeng when Mee-ami ees like dees, so enjoy. Siénten el ritmo, gringos ¡porque aquí no se sienten!*

The music sounded like the stuff grandpa played on the tape player when he sat in his armchair after working in the garage all day.

Have you ever had a Cuban sandwich? My aunt Juanita asked me.

Yeah, grandma makes them, sometimes.

My grandma told me that I was in for a surprise. We pulled up to a weathered-looking restaurant called La Cochina, in front, two men sat on wooden chairs playing dominos. My grandfather greeted them and went in to order the sandwiches while we waited in the car. Tío Ruperto asked me what I was learning in school. I told him that I was learning about Columbus in history class.

Qué aburrimiento ¿no? He said. I laughed and he spoke about how he used to ditch class when he was growing up in Cuba. I studied the lines of his cotton plaid shirt.

Ruperto was one of my worse student, my grandmother said.

You taught him? I said, astounded. It seemed like everyone from Cuba was connected. Ruperto feigned being offended and began defending himself. His hair was gray and smoothed back over his proud head with greasy pomade. His face was tanned and weathered, his eyes magnified by thick brown spectacles. His collar smelled of old cologne, the kind they sold at Sears. My grandfather walked out of the restaurant, called good evening to the men playing dominos, and handed Ruperto the paper bag. My grandfather tapped on the dashboard to the music.

No toca, mano, Ruperto said. Acabo de limpiarlo.

Perdóname, su excelencia, my grandfather said. He began telling a story about the day he had taken his little brother, Ruperto, to see a John Wayne movie, when they had lived in Miramar. He said Ruperto cried the entire ride to the movie theater because they had been late.

And then, my grandfather said in his gruff voice, we go in to watch the movie, and your uncle Ruperto want more candies. So I have to walk out of the movie and buy him candies. He was such a baby. My grandfather said sooch instead of such. Ruperto laughed it off.

I'm going to tell you something, sobrino, Ruperto said to me. I love cars. I used to race with Fangio in Cuba, I'm sure your grandma told you. I would normally never let anyone eat in one of my cars, especially this one, porque es mi preferido, but I will let you because you're my nephew and this is the first time you've have had a real sandwich in Miami. Don't spill any crumbs or te cojo por tus huevitos. His last comment frightened me, but I took the bag from him, pulled out a wrapped object, and tore the white paper to reveal a giant sandwich. Fresh, roasted pork and ham on Cuban bread with Swiss cheese, caramelized onions, and mustard. The sandwich was huge but I ate the whole thing, dripping grease all over my clean shirt. I finished before we got to the house. As we got out of the car, Ruperto announced, a mi sobrino le gustan mucho los Cuban sandwich.

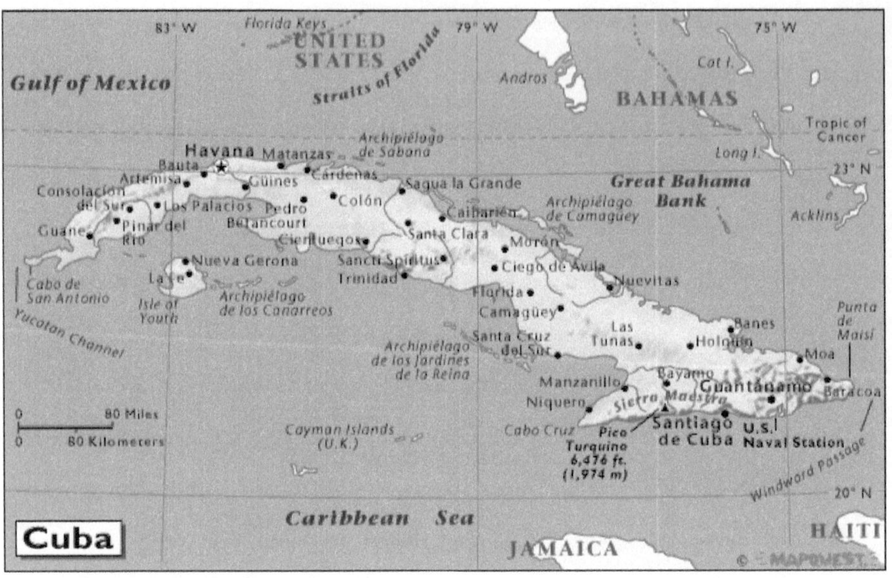

It all amounted to slips of paper. Some leftover invitations with notes and thank yous scribbled in the margins. A wedding certificate. A few photographs, black and white and curling at the edges. Items that meant nothing to anyone around there. There was a picture of the dead president next to a newly-wed couple. New tenants had stumbled over photographs once thought lost and then put them in a cardboard box. The papers sat in the box for a few weeks before someone recognized the woman in the picture. Teresa. He sealed them in a brown paper envelope and mailed them to a friend in México. The package was never opened or searched until it arrived in México and was given to a man named Javier, who checked the documents, remarked to himself about the former president, and addressed them to the Campesino's home. When the package arrived, it had been over ten years since either of them had seen the contents.

*****

Naperville, IL, United States of America, 1977

Teresa fingered her wedding ring. Despite the passage of a few years, they were still not accustomed to the plain silver wedding bands purchased upon their arrival in Miami. Their original wedding rings had been confiscated in the name of the Revolution. It was Thursday, her day off. She went to the sink to grab some clothes she had left to soak and hung them out to dry. She came back inside and began making eggs for her husband. He came out of the bedroom, smelling of cheap cologne, and wearing a white tank top and boxers. He ran his hand over his receding hairline.

¿Qué hay? ¿Facturas?

Dos. Y un paquete para ti. Viene de México.

The envelope felt heavy in Ricardo's hands. He went to the drawer and pulled out a pocket knife. The eggs sizzled. He sliced it open and pulled out a photo and a few slips of paper. He saw himself wearing a tuxedo, twenty-five years younger. His mouth was open in a cocky smile. He was careless. The Teresa that occupied the photo had little in common with the Teresa of that moment. Diamond earrings sparkled amid her long blonde hair and a pearl necklace ran around her cream-colored neck. Her eyes were both cold and warm, and her lips were held in a proud pose, not a smile, but a smirk of confidence. The pride of a woman who knew she was beautiful. Next to them was the President of Cuba, Carlos Prío Socarras. He was smiling as well. Teresa walked over and looked at the photograph. Her hair was in a bun and her lips were tight and untouched by lipstick. The knuckles of her hands were swollen from hours of folding sheets, emptying garbage cans, and typing. El pobre, she said. Carlos Prío Socarras, the former president, had shot himself in his home in Miami a few days earlier. It had been all over the news in Miami, but there was only a small blurb buried in the seventh page of the Chicago Tribune. Ricardo touched the white edge of the photograph. She noticed the grease underneath his fingernails.

Concho, Ricardo. Cuidado con las fotos. He put the photographs down on the otherside of the table and sat down to eat.

Carajo, vieja. Déjame quieto.

Teresa placed a plate of toast and eggs on the table. He broke the yolk open with his fork, dipped the dry white toast into the yellow liquid, and chewed it methodically. She placed a mug of bad coffee in front of him.

Gracias.

*****

Colombia Military Base, Cuba, 1947

Sometime after one o'clock on a Friday night, Ricardo Campesino was smoking outside a dancehall. It was one of the military's monthly dances. He was waiting for his friend Freddy; they were going to play blackjack at Carlo's. Despite many dances, both fast and slow, and the never-ending humidity, his beige uniform was not wrinkled and his charcoal-colored shoes had kept their sheen. He had lost two hundred the night before, and he intended to play it conservative tonight. Black Jack was the only game a man had a chance at beating the rake. Carlo's wasn't a casino, but a gambling houses had rakes, too.

Ricardo ashed his cigarette. Pedro Foyo came out of the club with his date and another couple.

Oye, Foyo, Ricardo said.

Foyo turned and called hello. He walked over with his date, a brunette with red lipstick.

Have you been here long? Pedro said. I didn't see—

And who are you? Ricardo said to the blonde standing next to Lourdes, Foyo's date.

She smiled at him inquisitively.

My name is Teresa Collazo, she said. I'm Lourdes' sister. Ricardo recognized Teresa's date from the Military Academy.

Where did you meet this clown? Ricardo asked, reffering to her date. He gave Ricardo a stern look and Ricardo said, Take it easy, mano. I'm just kidding.

We're just getting some fresh air, Lourdes said.

I'm going to get a bite to eat, but I'll be back, Ricardo said. He walked away, and without turning back, said, But seriously, Teresa. Where did you meet that clown?

*****

A light-skinned mulatto with a pencil mustache sang in a fluid tenor to a crowd of uniformed men and ladies. The horns swooned softly. Painting the room with his azure melody, the mulatto recalled the color of the wound in his father's chest, after they shot him. He sang just above a whisper, and three words later he was practically weeping, thinking about his mother, imploring the woman for whom the song was written, why had she had left him? It was a tango. The mulatto brought his voice down to a cold note, holding it tight in the back of his throat. The crowd fed off his sadness, moved with his cadence, and marveled at his pain. Sauntering into the dance hall as the song ended, Ricardo Campesino saw the dance floor come to a standstill, and the crowd became uncomfortable in the silence. The bongos and timbales sounded, signaling to Ricardo Campesino, and everyone around him, that they were still alive. The horns cut in, and everyone came back to life, having forgotten the sad song before, including the mulatto. Ricardo spotted Teresa on the otherside of the dancehall. He danced his way through the spinning couples, and whistled when he thought she was close enough to hear. She smiled and accepted his invitation, then they danced for a long while, and the mullato continued on the microphone. Another man tried to cut in at one point. You're going to have to fight me for her, Ricardo said. Afterwards he took her home, and then he went to play blackjack at Carlo's. He never told her, but she knew where he went after he dropped her off.

A few months later, Pedro Foyo asked Lourdes Collazo, the brunette with red lipstick, to marry him. She consented. Lourdes and her family, including her sister, Teresa, all went to live with Pedro Foyo on the Colombia Military Base, which was not far from Miramar. Pedro was a rising star in the Cuban military. As a student, he had received top marks in all his classes, graduated with a degree in engineering, and was steadily making his way up the ranks. His friends and fellow soldiers, like Ricardo Campesino, had to address him as captain.

Ricardo Campesino was following his own military track. A few years younger than his friend Pedro, he had enrolled in the military academy at the age of twenty at the behest of his father, General Ricardo Campesino. He received fair marks in most of his classes, especially military history, but had failed calculus. He was one of the fastest swimmers on the Academy's team, but his coach castigated him often for smoking.

*****

Teresa didn't like to drink, but Ricardo drank whiskey on the rocks. Ricardo's favorite singer was Beny Moré. Teresa's favorite song was "Unforgettable", because the first time she had heard it, when Nat King Cole played at the Tropicana, Ricardo had told her he was thinking of settling down. Marlon Brando had sat next to them that night and Ricardo had bought him six drinks. After he took Teresa home, he and Brando had gone to play Blackjack at Carlo's.

A few weeks later, Teresa found an evelope ay her door. It read:

I find no peace, and have no arms for war,
and fear and hope, and burn and yet I freeze,
and soar to heaven, lying on earth's floor,
and nothing hold, and all the world I seize.

My jailer opens not, nor locks the door,
nor binds me to here, nor will loose my ties;
Love kills me not, nor breaks the chains I wear,
nor wants me living, nor will grant me ease.

I have no tongue, and shout; eyeless, I see;
I long to perish, and I beg for aid;
I love another, and myself I hate.

Weeping I laugh, I feed on misery,
by death and life so equally dismayed:
for you, my lady, am I in this state.

She showed the poem to her sister, Lourdes.

This is from Ricardo Campesino?

Yes.

Ricardo Campesino wrote this himself?

No, he wrote me some other ones. Es Petrarco, creo.

It's a bit gloomy for a love poem, no?

Yes, it is a little disconcerting, but it's sweet nonetheless. The poem is full of paradoxes.

Paradoxes?

Yes.

Your boyfriend is either very clever and there is something beneath all this, or he's an idiot.

Don't be so harsh.

He could have at sent you something a little more romantic. Some *Shack-espeare*, or some Juan Boscán.

I like his choice. It shows originality. Did Foyo ever send you anything?

I think he sent me some *Shack-espeare*. Either way, I think you've had quite the effect on General Campesino's son.

General Campesino approached me the other day!

What? What did he say?

That Ricardo was acting strange after our date the other night. The general came riding toward me on that black horse of his. He greeted me and asked me what I'd done to his son. I was a little frightened at first, being addressed so directly. He said he didn't know what his son had been up to, that he had been hiding from him. I told him maybe his son didn't want him to know that he'd been drinking.

Loco Campesino. You've heard the stories about him in the Academy, Teresa. I don't know about him.

He's a wonderful man. He loves me and I love him.

Es un jugador, Teresa. And there are rumors about his family line.

There's rumors about our family line as well. We're all Cuban.

*****

They went to the movies often. With a chaperone, of course, usually her mother, Rosa, or her Uncle Francisco. One night Ricardo ran into an old friend at a club who took them to a bar. The writer Ernest Hemingway was commanding a table of people, each sipping from a communal drink. Teresa thought he was very charismatic, but found him a bit creepy. He had squeezed her arm, just above the elbow, when they met. Esse americano me cae mal, she had said to Ricardo.

Ricardo's father was eventually promoted to Chief of Staff of the Army after President Carlos Prío Socarrás was elected on July, 1 1948. Although Ricardo had not graduated from the military academy, he went to work for his father. He bought the ring that same year. It had a platinum band with tiny diamonds encrusted all the way around. Foyo took Lourdes and Teresa to New York City that year, and Ricardo went, as well. Teresa had never been to the United States before. They walked through Central Park and someone snapped a photograph of Teresa and Ricardo. There was a giant Coca-Cola billboard in the background. Ricardo wanted to ask her to marry him, but before he could ask her, he had to put it all on black, tell her every rotten thing that he'd done in his life, and hope that she'd still love him. He took her to a cafe on Broadway and 36th St.and explained to her that this was his confession. She nodded at him, but from the look in her eye he could tell that she was uneasy. He explained to her that his three vices of in life revolved around women, smoking, and gambling. He ripped a page out of a newspaper add and proceeded to write down his regrets, things he'd done before they'd met. He tried to explain them, having to pause after a couple sentences, in order to catch his breath, and make sure she wasn't completely outraged. She had a temper and it began to show, to the point that he was no longer comfortable speaking. There was a pause and he slipped her the torn piece of newspaper, on which he'd written two words: Mujeres. Debtos. She took it, crumpled it up, and threw it on the sidewalk.

You disgust me, she said, then she turned and went looking for her sister and Foyo, who were in a Gimbel's down the street. She didn't speak to him for the rest of the trip.

*****

There had been suspicions of a coup, but no one had any solid information. Ricardo's father, General Campesino, was sleeping in the arms of his wife, who later stole his money and a few of his watches after he was captured. Ricardo was asleep on the other side of the house, near the movie theatre. One of the men charged to guard the house was also asleep. There were no casualties at General Campesino's house, but a man was killed guarding the entrance to the base at Colombia. Ricardo was awakened at gunpoint and a bag was placed over his head. His father, the bigger target, was not assassinated, but placed on a plane to Miami. It was the morning of March, 10 1952. Fulgencio Batista overthrew the Prío government and the country went into shock. Teresa didn't learn the whereabouts of Ricardo for three weeks. She was forced to stay in her home for fear of violence.

President Carlos Prío Socarrás, the man in the Martí's wedding photo, was not a perfect president. He was, however, the last democratically elected leader of Cuba. He died on the fifth of April, 1977.

*****

Santiago, Republica Dominicana, 2005

She woke up early from the expensive sleep of hotel rooms. The sun peeked beneath the beige curtains and the air conditioner hummed. Teresa turned over and woke her two youngest granddaughters who slept next to her. Walking past the artful plate of fruit and Swiss chocolates in the adjoining suite, she woke her older grandchildren Ricky, Verónica, and Isabel. They protested loudly when Ricky's father, Richard, opened the blinds.

They were staying at the Grand Hilton Santiago in the Dominican Republic.

The family made its way down to the beach. Teresa watched the younger ones while her daughters-in-law lay in the sun. Later they left for tennis lessons and the outlet mall. Teresa stayed with the children.

In the evening, Teresa shuffled to the casino, where she spent no more than three hours. Estoy de vacaciones, she said defiantly when her younger son Carlos chided her. Her sons each gave her a daily gambling allowance of sixty dollars. I only play the machine, she said when her granddaughter, Angela, inquired.

Wearing a new outfit by that time of day, she said hello to the Edgar the bouncer who knew her by name. She made it a point to speak with all the employees, from the host of the restaurant to the Head of the Engineering Unit; her son Carlos was Director of the Caribbean for Hilton. It was her way of keeping tabs on him. If her son ignored her calls, she could call Tony, the Assistant Manager of the hotel or Miriam, his secretary.

She sat down on a purple stool and began dropping coins into the Pirate Booty slot machine. She smiled when it lit up and coins splashed down. She rarely won. She was not a gambler. Later she called her sisters to tell them about her day.

The beach was cool the next day. From the hotel balcony, the water looked clear. The family made its way down to the beach, the children scrambling excitedly. Ricky and his younger sister Angela looked like lobsters. The other three grandchildren, who lived in Puerto Rico, were bronzed and smelled of cocoa butter. The two sons, Richard and Carlos, shirtless and sporting ball caps, traded stories about business trips as they chewed on cigars. Richard had just bought a box of *Romeo y Julietas*. Checking themselves in the elevator mirror, the two wives, Raquel and Lynn, wore bikinis fresh out of catalogues. Teresa wore a loose cream beach dress with big brown sunglasses and a Panama hat. She looked not unlike a monk.

*****

Imported beer bottles dropped into sand that was as white as bone. It was against hotel policy to drink out of colored glass beer bottles on the beach but they did it anyway. The sons were sleepy. Teresa wiggled her toes in the sand as a waiter approached their group of umbrellas.

Esta playa es tan bella como la que visitábamos en Cuba, Teresa said.

Ay, Doña Teresa, said her daughter-in-law, Raquel. You need to go to Pinamar in Argentina. I used to go with my friends while I was in college. It is like this except more beautiful. The people are more beautiful as well.

Teresa nodded. The waiter asked Ricky if he wanted anything to drink.

Yo y mi hermana querémo dó piña colá. Vírgine, por favor.

Two virgin coladas coming right up, sir, the waiter said.

Ricky, where did you learn to speak like that? Ricky's aunt Fernanda asked. You drop your s's. His father Richard agreed. No one in their family spoke that way. Ricky blushed and said he didn't know. His sister hadn't understood any of the Spanish and asked what they were talking about.

He sounds like a jíbaro, his aunt Fernanda said, laughing.

Or a guajiro, his father said.

Or a poblano, his uncle said.

The family settled into the laze that accompanies imported beer and over-priced club sandwiches. They hovered in a state between sun and sleep, as if hanging precariously, vulnerable to the slightest disturbance.

Teresa said, *One time your grandpa make love to me on this beach!*

For the first time, everyone noticed the sound of the tide rising and falling, and then burst into raucous laughter. Teresa's son Richard offered a postulation on post-menopausal syndrome. Ricky yelled out, *Gross*, and his cousins laughed. Her statement had been a blatant lie. No one in the family had been to the Dominican Republic except for Carlos, who had come for business. Neither Teresa, nor her deceased husband had ever been to that beach.

Cuidado, Mami. Carlos said. You're going to traumatize the children.

Déjala, his wife, Fernanda said, laughing. This isn't the old times. She's a sexual being. Teresa's husband had been dead for seven years.

Mira a esse viejito allí, Richard said, gesturing at a dark wrinkled man wearing a Speedo. He's giving you the eye, Mami. Now's your chance. The dark wrinkled man smiled at them. Teresa fiddled with her silver ring, which she wore on a necklace.

Her family continued to make fun of her.

Concho, she said finally, Déjanme quieto. She stood up from her chair.

Where are you going? her granddaughter, Angela, asked. Why is everyone yelling?!

Cuídan a sus hijos. ¡Me voy al Casino!

I was alone in the kitchen when my grandfather Ricardo came in the garage door.

Vén, Ricky. Tú hermana nació.

I sprinted to turn off the television, wearing nothing but whitey-tighties. My grandfather poured himself a glass of tomato juice and sat down at the kitchen table. I sprinted past him again, and went up the stairs to get dressed. I ran past baby pictures, wedding photos, and pictures of people I'd heard about, but never met. There was a picture of me as a baby, dressed as a clown. I grabbed a green crewneck, threw it on, and slipped on some jean shorts. I ran back down the stairs to the door. My grandfather stared out the window as he washed out the dirty glass. He brushed his plaid shirt and followed me out the door.

Is mom OK?

Sí, está bien.

I jumped into the passenger seat and strapped on my seat belt before my grandfather reached the car. I tapped my fingers on the dash as I watched my grandfather lumber towards the car in a red and blue plaid shirt. He sat down and began smoothing his white and grey hair with a pocket comb. He slipped the key into the ignition and turned the car on. I switched on the radio to a favorite station.

What does she look like?

No sé. No la vi, pero tu abuela me dijo que parece mucho a ti.

We pulled out of the driveway and headed out of the neighborhood. I tried to remember how long it had been since my parents had first told me about her. The idea had seemed exciting; I had always wanted an older brother. A baby seemed almost as good. My grandfather was extremely calm, given what had happened.

How many times have you done this? I asked. My grandfather continued to watch the road.

Muchas.

Were you ever scared?

Claro que sí.

Was grandma scared?

Un poco. Tu abuela es muy fuerte. Tiene mucho fé.

Were you there when I was born?

Sí, estuve. ¿Sabes en que hospital naciste?

One in Chicago.

Nortwestern Memorrial Hópital.

We stopped at a traffic light at a busy intersection. My grandfather seemed tired. He had been having pains and wake up in the middle of the night. My grandmother had been worried about him for the last couple weeks.

Parece que tu abuelo está enfermo.

Why do you say that, grandma? I asked.

He gets tired easier than he used to. He does not spend so much time in the garage.

Maybe he's sick of it.

Conozco Ricardo más que nadie. Soy su esposa. Trabajé veinte años en un hospital. Temo que tenga cáncer.

I know.

So what are you going to do?

We make an appointment to see doctor. We see.

Since then, my grandfather had been gone to the hospital a few times, but the last time they had sent him all the way to Loyola, near Chicago. They were worried that he might have cancer.

The only time I was ever scare, was when your aunt Maria was born. She was premature, my grandfather said, as we drove to the hospital. You could hold her in one hand, she was so small.

Grandma told me about that once.

Tuvimos mucho suerte. I don't like to think about it now, because everyone was so worry. Your grandmother especially. She used to spend half her time in church and half her time in the hospital, praying. It never bother me, though. I knew Maria would be OK.

How did you know?

I knew she would be fine. My grandfather pushed in a tape cassette and a woman began to sing in Spanish.

And Kristen is fine?

She is fine.

We pulled into the parking lot of Edwards Hospital, where my grandmother had worked as a nurse's assistant for almost twenty years.

*****

My grandmother had a degree in education from the University of Havana, but that had meant little in Illinois. The reason my grandparents had moved to Naperville in the first place was because jobs had been available. My grandfather had worked at a warehouse at Bell Labs, while my grandmother went to work at the hospital. When she began working there, no one could pronounce her name correctly, so they called her "tootsie" instead of Teresa. Among her many duties, tootsie fluffed pillows, washed the shitty asses of the bed-ridden, and did paper work. During the seventies, she began using a state-of-the-art IBM desktop computer. She had a lot of trouble with technology; she preferred a typewriter, even with sticky keys. During a busy Wednesday, she had trouble remembering the various codes to retrieve files, quit programs, or save files. She tried several keys, but the obstinate green message repeated the same annoying message: ERROR. Her friend Doris came over to help her.

Oh, Tootsie, Doris said. Why did they ever put you in front of a computer?

I don't know, tootsie said, smiling in embarrassment. After that she started carrying a notebook with her and writing notes about which keys to press and when. She had the practiced hand of an ex-school teacher and wrote in an elegant cursive. She wondered how her students were doing. Perhaps the revolution had been good for them? Her supervisor called her and as she rose from her desk, she knocked over her glass of water onto some patient charts.

Fidel Castro, she said, under her breath.

What Tootsie? Her supervisor said.

She found doctors to be the most pompous people she had ever met in her life.

Doctor Stevens me gritó en frente de todas las nurses, she told my grandfather one night. Nunca vi una persona tan pesado en mi vida. Es una falta de educación.

Es un hijo de puta, my grandfather said.

No habla así en frente de mí.

By the time she retired, my grandmother had acquired an encyclopedic knowledge for diseases, maladies, and even some psychological conditions.

Always wash your hands before you eat dinner, she told me, often. E. Coli is a very dangerous bacteria and it can result in vomiting and sometime worse thing.

Ricky, she said another time. The kids are not having sex yet are they? Have you heard of Syphilis? It is a sexually-transmitted disease caused by bacteria. Most people do not have symptoms, but if gone untreated, it can lead to mental disorder.

*****

Her tiny body was much lighter than I thought it would be. My parents had let choose her name: Angela. My grandfather gave a watch that day. A silver Rolex. I put it to my ear and listened to the ticks. I never wore it though, because it made think of poor people in Latin America.

Sweat pooled in his armpits and dripped from his socks, down his shins to his knees. Ricardo opened his eyes. His mouth was cloudy in the morning humidity and his tongue tasted like whiskey and Chesterfields. He was thirsty. He wiped the grime from his eyelids and seconds passed before his eyes focused, taking in the deserted game room. He was lying on a sofa, legs sprawled against the wall and still wearing the white suit and shoes from the night before. Scuff marks crowded the walls, where his feet had been. The table at the center of the room was bare. For a second, he heard the sounds of chips clicking, cards shuffling, ice cubes splashing and clinking into glasses. The smell of smoke and hot, sticky air. The sounds of póquer, black jack, ruleta, dados, y mucho más.

Me cago en diez, he said, to no one. Qué hora é? The sun peeked in through the white shutters, letting him know how late it was, which made him realize that his wife, Teresa, would be waiting for him, deathly worried, and above all, irritated. It couldn't have been later than ten, he thought. He instinctively reached for his right pocket. His watch was gone. He tapped his chest above his heart, feeling for his wallet. It was light. He reached into his jacket, slipped out the worn leather holder, and furrowed it open. No bills. Thirteen cents American. Carajo. Teresa me va a matar. He remembered arriving there sometime after two, but nothing after that.

He stood up. The blood rushed from his head and he felt dizzy for a moment. Thinking of Teresa and what she would say, he unbuttoned his shirt, and slipped his wrinkled bow tie into his watchless pocket. What the hell was the time? He crouched and reached for his ankle holster. Still there. Teresa didn't like the fact that he carried, but after having been in the Military Academy, he couldn't go anywhere without a revolver. Besides, everyone was armed anyway. How else was he supposed to protect his family? He took off the jacket, swung it over his shoulder, and left the room. The air was cool on his belly so he decided to take his shirt off as well. He felt better, but it was still hotter than hell.

¿Hay alguién en casa? ¿Félix? ¿Rosita? He walked into the kitchen. It was empty except for a mango on a cutting board. He looked around again. No one. He pulled a pairing knife from a fissure in a wood block and sharpened it on a whetstone. The scraping gave him a headache. The mango was a little on the green side, but it felt ripe. He plopped it down on the table and slit it lengthwise, along the flat side next to the seed. He turned it on the other side and split the two halves of the mango. He left them there and walked out of the steamy kitchen sucking on the mango seed. The pulp was fleshy and sweet. Juice pearled on the hairs of his mustache and dribbled down his chin. He turned the seed around in his hand, sucking it dry with his lips and his teeth. Mangoes were great for hangovers.

A black man was working in the garden. It was Pedrito the houseboy.

Oye, Pedrito. ¿Dónde está Félix?

Hola, Sr. Campesino. How are you feeling today? Sr. Félix left early this morning to visit his brother's plantation in Camaguey.

Pedrito, I didn't give you my pocket watch last night, did I? Ricardo slid his thumbnail between his two front teeth. The mango fibers made his gums itchy. Pedrito laughed.

Sí, Sr. Campesino. You gave it to me and told me to not let you gamble no more.

¿Lo tienes?

No, Sr. Campesino. No lo tengo.

Why not? My father gave me that watch, Pedrito. It is very important to me.

No, Sr. Campesino. You came back and told me you were kidding. And then you took the watch. Pedrito averted his gaze.

Y lo perdí… Qué estupidez.

No es tan malo, Sr. Campesino. Cada día se le presenta a una nueva oportunidad.

De estropear, Pedrito. De estropear. You don't know where my hat is, do you?

I think you left it in your car, Sr. Campesino, so you wouldn't bet it.

Gracias, Pedrito. He left him and walked around the house to his car, which was parked in the driveway. He ran over his schedule for today in his mind. He loved that watch. It was a Swiss watch with a gold base, and a silver dimensional design of a tiger. His father had given it to him when he had entered the military academy. He walked to the other side of the house where his car was parked. A blue Packard was coming slowly down the road. It stopped and the man stared at him through the window. The driver was a pale-faced with bags under his eyes, and lips and fingernails stained with nicotine. Ricardo recognized him.

Sr. Campesino, he said through discolored teeth. I think we've met before.

Yes, I'm sorry, Ricardo said. Could you remind me of your name? Esteban?

Santiago. Santiago Markov. Ricardo tensed up at the mention of his name.

Markov? Is that Russian?

Yes, my father emigrated after the Great War, he said, as he took off his hat. He was bald, except for thin lines of grey hair, greased down the back of his skull.

My family came around the same time from the Canary Islands, Ricardo said.

Yes, well, listen Sr. Campesino. I work for an Eli Steinmetz. Markov wore a green shirt with stains on the armpits.

¿Y qué?

I don't want to alarm you, Sr. Campesino, he said, pulling a toothpick from his pocket. I'm just a numbers guy. I'm no street tough. I don't doubt that someone of your social position could easily pay his debts, but I just wanted to let you know to be careful, Sr. Campesino.

Vete a la mierda. I haven't been late on a payment in five years.

I'm not trying to intimidate you, Sr. Campesino. We're friends right?

I can take care of myself.

Think about it, Markov said, picking at his gums. His eyelids and lips were pink, which contrasted with the pastiness of his face and forehead, making him look like some kind of rodent-fish. He dug into his gums with the toothpick, causing them to bleed. He continued to speak. You've got a family, now, Sr. Campesino. I've got a little boy at home, too, and I'd never want to put him in danger. At the mention of his family, Ricardo pulled the revolver from his ankle holster and pointed it at Markov.

Listen to me you son of a bitch. Stay away from my family.

Jesus Christ, Markov said, throwing his hands up. Put the gun down. This isn't what you think. Put the gun down. Ricardo lowered the gun, but refrained from holstering it. Markov wheezed, and touched his chest with his hands. Blue veins stood out on his pasty temples. Ricardo wondered how someone could live in Havana and not have any color.

This isn't the old days, Sr. Campesino. Gambling is a serious business, now. We run things right since the Americans came in, he said, lighting a cigarette and taking in a breath of smoke. Vegas standards. Big things are happening, Sr. Martí. They've kicked the juice up two points on you, and if you're late on the payment, people are going to start asking questions. I know your father was a big shot, but Batista doesn't owe you anymore favors. Don't think you can call on someone at the top to bail you out this time.

I would still be in the military if it weren't for you. Don't think I've forgotten.

Ancient history, Sr. Campesino. Perhaps if you had been timelier with your payments, I wouldn't have had to visit your superior. Ricardo didn't answer. He stared at Markov, seething with hatred, yet unable to act on it. Markov spoke again. Yes, well, your father doesn't run things anymore, Sr. Campesino. Too bad for you. From what I've heard, Batista's men had a gun to your head before you woke up. Your father should have bothered to hire a better bodyguard. Perhaps someone who graduated from the Military Academy. You're lucky they didn't kill you.

You stupid fuck. Do you think Batista has the power to kill a white man on this island? The upper class never would have stood for it. What do you think the Americans would have done?

You seem to have a penchant for debating history, Sr. Campesino. But that's all it is. Ancient History. The question is: can you afford to continue on this losing streak?

Qué te follen, Ricardo said, holstering his gun. He walked away from Markov and got into the car. He could still see him in the rearview mirror as he turned the corner. His stained green shirt and pale head. What a devious bastard. Ricardo had been on a losing streak lately. Since Batista had taken over the country, his father had been living in exile in Miami, with one of Ricardo's brothers, and Ricardo had taken a job as a paralegal. He couldn't stand the paperwork, and bureaucrats made him sick, but there was nothing else he could do. He knew a fair amount of people who were still in the military, including Foyo, but he himself had never graduated from the Academy, and had no desire to start again at the bottom. Under Batista's regime, nonetheless. He used to just play black jack, but now with the boredom at work, he found himself playing roulette, for hours, and betting on horses, which he never used to do. Markov had been referring to debts on horse racing.

Ricardo drove down stone roads, past pinkish stone houses, tapping his hand on windowsill. He drove through the downtown, through the smells of beer, fried food, and fumes. He drove by the Calle Industria, where José Martí had grown up, and Ricardo started singing one of his poems, which put him at ease. His father had made him memorize them as a child, and he repeated them from time to time, when he was nervous. A son of Cuba must know the words of its greatest patriot, his father, the former general, had said. He used to wish he was a descendent of José Martí. A guy who was too good do shit that he did, like gambling his father's money away on horses.

El alma trémula y sola
Padece al anochecer:
Hay baile; vamos a ver
La bailarina española

Ricardo appreciated the ballet. He wasn't some kind of dandy or coxcomb, but he liked the dancers. He didn't know very much about the ballet, but having been a child of wealth, his mother had forced him and his brothers to attend a few shows while he was growing up, before she got sick. There was something about the fluid movement of the painted-up chiquillas. They looked so angelic. He had secretly enjoyed the show, but never said a word to anyone. Afterwards, his mother had taken him backstage to meet the director, an old Russian woman. She had introduced him to the star ballerina, a Spanish woman from Sevilla. From the audience, she had looked no older than fifteen. Thin, flat-chested, and made up like a fairy. She was an angel. When he met her, he was shocked by how big her legs were, like a horse's. She had taken off her slippers and he could see the bunions on her feet. She was actually much older than he had thought, *as old as his mother*. After that, he tried to forget that he'd met her. He preferred the memory of the baby girls, wafting safely like gulls on the stage. He wished things were still as simple.

He pulled up onto his street, which was in the Miramar neighborhood, not far from the country club. His two boys were in front of the house. Javier was on his knees with his hands over his mouth. Little Ricky was standing behind him with his hands on Javier's shoulder. Javier was crying.

¿Qué pasó aquí? He said to Little Ricky, who was standing over his brother, hugging him.

Nada, papi. Un accidente. Javier took his hand away from mouth and there was blood.

Hestabamo lanzando con mansahh. Jiqui me pegó con una bateria. Me duehe hucho, papi. Herdí mees hientes. His top four teeth were in his hand and his top lip was swollen. He had trouble pronouncing words through spit and blood.

Ricky, are you crazy? Why would you throw a battery at your brother?

Daddy, I'm sorry. I didn't mean to, Daddy. We were throwing apples, and I didn't think, I just found it in the yard and threw it. Please.

Where's your mother?

She left a while ago. Tía Lourdes had her baby. Daddy, I'm sorry. Don't teach me a lesson.

Ricky, don't lie to me. Tía Lourdes isn't due for another two months. He wanted to smack his son in the face so he took him by the collar and brought him into the garage. Javier stopped crying and watched them. Ricardo was still shirtless, carrying his jacket on his shoulder, and pulling his son along. He threw his clothes onto a bench in the garage and said, Drop your pants, hijo. Little Ricky was quiet, and slowly he slipped his white shirt over his chubby head. He pulled down his pants, revealing his tiny white buttocks and thimble penis. Ricardo removed his belt from his pants and cracked it. He bent his son over on the bench, and struck him three times. His son trembled each time, but didn't make a sound, which pleased his father.

Now tell me, Ricardo said, looping his belt. Where's your mother?

I told you, Daddy, he said, in a hollow voice. She's at the hospital. The baby came early so mami had to rush to the hospital.

All right, get your brother cleaned up. Have him wash his mouth out. We can get his face fixed while we're there.

*****

The baby looked like an alien fetus. She was smaller than his hand, with arms as thin as his pinky, wrinkled like an old man's. One eye was closed. Her head was misshapen, and despite the tube in her mouth, she breathed and sucked pathetic breaths. Her face reminded Ricardo of one of the characters from las Pinturas Negras de Goya. She looked both old and new at the same time. Less than a kilogram. María de los Milagros. They didn't think she would live, but they were going to try.

Lourdes was still sleeping. Foyo was marching back and forth in the waiting room. Teresa came out of the delivery room.

Teresa, he said, dumbly. He moved to kiss her, but she moved away from him. His mustache brushed her nose. She sniffed.

Where the hell were you, Ricardo?

Amor, he said, grabbing her hand, which was in a fist. I was at Félix's. I got tired and fell asleep.

Borracho, she said, almost shouting it. Estabas borracho. Don't lie to me, Ricardo.

Amor, I came home, didn't I? I was a little late, that's all. Her hair was in a bun and her eyes made him feel uncomfortable. What more did she want from him?

This is all I'm going to say to you, Ricardo. My sister almost died today. Her baby probably will die. I had to leave the kids at home, and Javier lost four teeth, because you were out bebiendo y jugando black jack con los hombres. We're not in our twenties anymore, Ricardo. If you keep doing this, I'm going to leave you.

*****

Ricardo ashed his third cigarette and asked for another cortadito. He liked the café, despite its dinginess. The other ones were full of vacationing Americans, waiting for Hemingway, and commenting on how wonderful everything was. The heat. The beaches. The natives. He didn't know what the hell was so wonderful. It was hotter than shit, and the government collapsed every decade or so. He checked his cigarette case, which was empty, so he stood up and went to the bathroom. The wall tiles were light blue and the toilet was small and white, shoes squeaking on the wet floor. He turned the faucet on and looked at himself in the mirror. His face was haggard but clean-shaven except for a black mustache. His grey fedora was tipped low to his eyes. He brushed his navy sports coat and retucked his shirt into his tailored slacks. He spit polished his leather shoes until the beige vamps were clean and the tongues were white and shiny.

3 kilos, he thought to himself. Pedro had picked a good name for her, María de los Milagros. He walked back to his table, smiling. The baby was alive.

He was waiting for Pedro, who was uncharacteristically late. Ricardo felt his mouth water at the thought of another cigarette. He would ask Pedro for one. He preferred Cuban tobacco, but Pedro smoked Chesterfields. I'll make do, he thought.

Pedro turned the corner and searched the café. Ricardo waved to him.

Oye, Capitán Pedro. Pedro was in a beige uniform, just like an American G.I. He was skinny with a hooked nose, which made him look like a bird. Manuel the waiter, in a sopping guayabera, brought out two cortaditos. Ricardo thanked him.

You don't have to call me that. We've been family for almost a year, now.

Habit, Ricardo said, looking away.

You know you only had six more months in the Academy. You could have appealed the decision.

No me habla deso, Ricardo said.

I'm sorry I brought it up.

There was a pause, which might have been awkward had Manuel not brought out two espressos, for which Ricardo tipped him a few pesos. Pedro began recounting his schedule for the last couple days, what had been happening in his department. What the hell is he talking about his job for? Ricardo thought. He wanted to ask Pedro about his daughter, but he felt self-conscious. She was his niece after all, but Ricardo did not like to be overly emotional. He couldn't stop thinking about her since he had first seen her those few months ago. Since then he had visited her twice a week, bringing her a present each time. Blankets. Pink booties. A glass bottle.

¿No trajiste los otros reyes? Pedro's wife, Lourdes, had said to him.

Me llamo Santo Clau, he had said, laughing. He hadn't been able to visit her the last two weeks because he had been so busy filing property claims. The Americans were buying. He had called Foyo to have lunch so he could find out about the kid.

So how is she? Ricardo asked.

Who?

Maria. Your kid.

Oh. She's… She's fine. I can't believe it myself. I'm sure Teresa told you. She came down with a fever last week, but now she's fine.

You could hold her in the palm of your hand when she was born.

Don't say that, Pedro said. I don't want to think about it.

Celia said she has a little bit of fuzz on her head now too?

María the bald miracle, Pedro said.

And there have been no other complications? Ricardo said. What do the doctors say? She doesn't need another surgery?

Everything's fine. To think the hell Norma went through. I can't remember how many cigarettes I smoked that night. And now it's so…calm.

This place is anything but calm, Ricardo said. Can I have a cigarette?

Pedro nodded and pulled out a gold case. Ricardo took one and struck a match.

This is a Corona.

Chesterfields make me think of that night, Pedro said.

Me too.

Pedro excused himself to urinate. An old man called to him and he went over to say hello. Ricardo signaled Manuel for another cortadito and promised himself this would be his last one until dinner. His doctor said he had high blood pressure from too much coffee and cigarettes. He checked his watch; he would have to get going soon. He had promised to take his little brother to the new John Wayne movie. Pedro returned.

Was that Alberto Ferrer you were talking to? Ricardo asked.

Yeah. He looks good. He looks healthy.

Yeah, Foyo said. They sat in silence, each staring in one direction. The street was fairly quiet.

I saw you on Sunday, Pedro said.

So? Ricardo said. I go to church sometimes.

Is it true what they've been saying about you?

What?

That Ricardo Campesino has finally calmed down, Pedro said. That you're playing less blackjack, staying home more.

Malicious lies.

Lourdes says it's because of Maria. Teresa told her that you've been going to church more.

Ricardo wiped his mustache with his palm and then said, I've been going for the last month and a half. I only missed once because I was tired one morning. I hit a streak playing blackjack the night before. Teresa damn near talked my ear off afterwards.

What's this sudden change? I thought you were an agnostic?

I don't know.

So it was María, Pedro said. Ricardo laughed.

I can't believe it either, Pedro said. I don't know how María survived. But I thank God everyday.

Did I tell you I dropped out of the masons? Ricardo said.

What did your father say? Did you call him?

He gave me some shit like he always does, but it was fine. I'm a grown man; I can make my own decisions.

What made you decide to quit? Your brothers are in it too right?

It was just a bunch of bull shit. All of it. To initiate you, they put you in a coffin, close the lid, and lower you into a pit for five minutes. You're supposed to be 'resurrected in fraternity' when you come back out.

No resurrection for you?

No. I was screaming for about two minutes when I was in there. Then my voice went hoarse. I came out and I was just happy to be alive. That was a year ago, and since then I've been lucky enough to get sauced a couple of times, and go to meetings and listen to a bunch of hollow rhetoric about brotherhood and fraternity. It's a drinking club. Plain and simple. If I'm going out drinking, I'll do it with my friends, I don't need a cult.

You're missing out now. None of the Masons will show up to your funeral when you die, now that you've quit.

Good riddance, Ricardo said.

You sound so negative.

I am, Ricardo said, laughing. I don't need a big funeral. A simple one will be fine. Let my father have the big show when he finally kicks the bucket.

Do you like church?

Not really.

You still don't believe in God?

I believe in María, Ricardo said.

What do you do once you're there? Pedro asked. I can't see you praying.

That's my business, Ricardo said, finishing the last sip of the cortadito. Life is too short to spend all this time talking about sad things.

Well, some people need it, Pedro said. They need it to help them get by.

I believe in something, Ricardo said. But right now, these cortaditos are enough to get me by.

You should cut down on those, Pedro said. Your hand is shaking.

They said goodbye to one another. Ricardo went to look for his black Chevrolet. He stopped at a street vendor and bought some plátanos maduros from a buck-toothed Chinaman named Felipe. It seemed like all the chinos in Havana were named Felipe. He ate them with a tooth pick, chewing them slowly, savoring them. His mother used to make them when he was a child, and Teresa made them as well, but she could never seem to get the flavor right. The Chino had done a proper job, though. They were sweet and flavorful, smelling of the oil and sugar they had been fried in. It looked like a storm was coming.

He drove down the Malecón, which was beginning to flood. The waves battered the small stone wall that separated the famous boulevard from the sea, and someone was doing donuts behind him on the road. The sounds of the oncoming storm comforted him, reminding him of his mother, of the night that she'd jumped in the pool at the dinner party, looped out on pills. It had stormed that night too. He laughed to himself. Clouds gathered and the waters furied, and after a few minutes of thought, Ricardo came to the realization that things were probably not going to get any easier. He decided to get on with it. He drove all the way there, patting the envelope in the passenger seat, as if it would disappear if he stopped touching it. He walked into the casino, brushing the rain off his hat, then took a side door, nodding hello to the man at table in the next room. He went through another doorway, and found Markov.

Tengo el dinero, Ricardo said. Estoy hecho.

¿Cómo mantendré a mis hijos y nietos? Quería comprarme un yacht, también. Markov laughed at his own jokes. Ricardo smiled. He had been thinking about the movies, because he still had to take his little brother to see the new John Wayne picture, so it didn't take him long to think of a come back.

Frenly miye darleenh, I don geev a dam.

■■

Needle in the Hay

(Cousin José {middle, w/ the Green Day shirt} at Woodstock 1994)

When I was eleven years old, my grandmother walked into the garage and found my grandfather dead, lying in a pool of blood. He had recovered from cancer a few months earlier. At the time, I had been learning about Greek mythology in school, and during those first few days after his death, myths colored my understanding of him and my family. My grandfather had first gone to the oncologist after having noticed blood in his stool. After he died, I tried to write a story about his battle with intestinal cancer. Here is the description of him in the hospital:

> He lay on his back. His hands were unmarked and his feet were cold. His neck was in some sort of collar, and there was a tube shoved into his throat, breathing for him. Another tube went into his arm. There was a sensor attached to his left index finger, and another tube ran under the white sheet to his genitals. A sterile white bandage covered part of his stomach and suddenly the room smelled like shit.

I had always associated honor and manhood with my grandfather. I took pride in the fact that he had served in the army, and made a new life for his family in America. My grandfather had been a sturdy man; a carpenter. The first time he showed weakness in front of me was when he shit himself in the hospital. After he recovered, I was convinced that he would live until he was one hundred.

You're grandpa is one tough son of a bitch, my father remarked with pride at the dinner table. My grandmother made chicken noodle soup, but my grandfather wasn't allowed to have any because of the salt content.

He was lifting a hundred pound oak chest when his heart gave out. The vessels in his brain exploded, and he died instantly. As he fell to the floor, his right temple slammed against a metal clamp attached to the counter, leaving a depression in his skull. My grandmother found him with a halo of blood around his body and the chest at his side. My father saw the body, but I had to imagine it. I had seen *Saving Private Ryan*; I knew what violence looked like, but I was watching Saturday morning cartoons with my mother when the phone rang. My father rushed out of the house. My plate of strawberry pop tarts lay cold and untouched on the table.

Papi se cayó, he had said. I waited in the kitchen in terror, walking the white tiles, making sure not to step on the cracks. I chewed the flesh of my inner cheek as black fantasies crept through my mind, visions of my grandfather brain-dead or paralyzed from the waist down. However desolate my fantasies were, I knew that he was alive. When my father returned, I couldn't talk. *Is he dead?* I wanted to ask, but my mouth was locked shut. *Is he dead?* I opened my mouth, but before I said the words, my father nodded and hugged me, telling me it would be all right. I writhed out of his grip ran to the bathroom. My tears tasted like the salt water my grandmother forced me to gargle when I had a sore throat.

During the five-minute car ride to my grandparents' home, I tried to imagine my grandmother's face. She would be crying. I had never seen her cry. We pulled up to the gray house that my grandparents had moved into the summer before, smaller than the one on Green St., but much closer to ours. The driveway and the curb were crowded with SUVs and minivans. The family was there. My father said a priest had been there earlier, but he was gone. I ran to the garage. It was locked. As I walked to the other side of the house, I was surprised to see my cousin José sitting on the porch, sipping on a flask. He looked like a rock star, or a gas station attendant. It was the first time I had seen him in two years. He exchanged an awkward embrace with my father, and commented on how much I had grown. I barely remembered José. I knew about him because his mother, my father's cousin, complained to my grandmother about him. He lacked direction in life, which his mother attributed to the fact that he had never been confirmed. His head was shaved, and his face was thin. He had been living in Europe and had obviously not been eating much. As we entered the house, my father muttered something under his breath about money and drugs.

My grandmother was waiting. She pulled me close to her and whispered into my ear. Her breath smelled like onions. Your grandpa is in heaven now. Pray to San Juan Bosco, Ricky. Él te ayuda. He helps all the children. Her hair was thin and disheveled, unrecognizable from her usual hairdo. Her face was contorted into a mask of grief: the skin red, the eyelids swollen. I hugged her and, as I stepped back, noticed her thin little wrists and knobby hands, covered in age spots and stove burns.

San Juan Bosco was the patron saint of children and my grandmother's favorite saint. She had repeated his biography to me many times in her funny accent, each time using the same words that I did not understand. I had memorized the whole of his biography as if it were a prayer.

San Juan Bosco was a sensualist and an atheist, who rejected the world as God had created it, solely because of the suffering of children. One day he had a vision of Christ standing before him, dressed in the clothing of the time. A short while after, someone came across him kneeling on the ground and noticed that his hands were bleeding. He joined the priesthood and built orphanages to help children. He died a martyr, crucified upside down like St. Peter. Gracias a San Juan Bosco.

I usually accepted what my grandmother told me, but at that moment, I refused to believe that the spirit of a dead priest could help me. I rejected him and his biography. My grandfather was dead, and my suffering was my own. I went upstairs to the room my grandmother kept for me. The scented comforter had white elephants in purple suits with crowns on their heads. The white walls were decorated with only two photographs: one of me at Disney World, and another of a brown-skinned priest: *San Juan Bosco.* I turned on the television. A music video was on, something sentimental:

So take the photographs and still frames in your mind
G C9 Dsus4 G
Hang them on a shelf in good health and good time
G C9 Dsus4 G
Tattoos and memories and dead skin on trial
Em Dsus4 C9 G
For what it's worth, it was worth all the while
Em Dsus4 C9 G

It's something unpredictable, but in the end is right
Em G Em G
I hope you had the time of your life.
D Em Dsus4 G

I mouthed the first lines, and then began to sing, my voice raspy and hollow. It was a song by Green Day, one of my favorite bands. I thought that the words might ease the pain; I liked the song and had listened to it many times, but in the wake of this new terror, it seemed more like a jingle than an ode. I tried to watch the video, thinking that it would make me feel better, but the television hurt my eyes, and gave me a headache. I rose from the bed and as I stared at the photo of the dead priest, a fury rose in my heart. I threw the remote control at the picture of San Juan Bosco, shattering it. A mass of glass and double-A batteries littered the carpet.

*****

Light shone through the red-stained glass, the color of Christ's blood. I sat in the pew next to my grandmother in the church of Sts. Peter and Paul, a gothic building with high ceilings. Someone was delivering a sermon about my grandfather, but I wasn't listening. The priest had marched around my closed grandfather's coffin with the incense, and sprayed us with water. José sat behind us. I noticed the incense because it cancelled out the smell of whiskey on José's breath

I stared at the various ornaments in the church; the stained glass windows and the statues. On one side of the church stood a massive statue of St. Peter, and on the other side, his counterpart, St. Paul. Peter clutched the keys to heaven and hell, while Paul held a long scroll and quill. One man held God's wrath; the other His reason. They both had large, flowing beards. As I came to the realization that the statues were almost identical, my grandmother cried out, yelping in high-pitched exertions like a dog. I turned away from the bearded statues and wrapped my arms around her. I felt a flash of shame, and looked behind me at the congregation, embarrassed.

I had always been an earnest Catholic. My cup of faith, to use an old metaphor, had been small, but I soon discovered it was fragile as well. The walls of my imagination had been defined by the Benevolent One, whose existence had been professed to me through red glass, carved stone, and splattered ink. The images were powerful, and the stories majestic, but I could no longer believe them. I walked up the aisle to receive the sacrament, between the identical gray stares of St. Peter and St. Paul, licking a cut in my mouth.

*****

We had swallowed the communion wafers, and it was time to follow the coffin out of the church. My grandmother walked next to me, draped in black; my arms ached from holding her. I wondered if I would always have to take care of her and protect her. The rows of people watching us made me think of a parade I had once been forced to march in. The marble floor was a road, and the coffin was a float. There were distractions all around us, but my grandmother and I walked out of the church alone.

"On Eagle's Wings" was playing. I had picked the song.

*****

Our teachers would bring us to church so that the priests could show us around. Explain the different ornaments. Give us lectures on the Stations of the Cross lining the walls. During the Dark Ages, the peasants could not read the Bible, so the priests told the story of Christ through paintings and stained glass. The Stations depicted the sufferings of

Christ before he died and was resurrected.

Father, does the Lord forgive those who aren't Christian? Someone asked.

The Lord forgives all, he said. But only those who repent can be forgiven. My class settled in front of the piano, near the statue of St. Peter. I preferred him to Paul, because he was more impulsive and head-strong, like me. The priest seemed to prefer him as well, because he mimicked the statue's pose. Mrs. Griggs, the pianist, began to play and the boys' choir sang "On Eagles Wings."

And he will raise you up, on Eagle's Wings
Bear you on the breath of dawn

And make you to shine like the sun

And hold you in the palm of his hand

I imagined that God's giant hand held me. I imagined that He made me to shine like the sun. I was moved by the power of the words. Not wanting to be seen, I stuck my head in my lap. One of my classmates noticed, but she didn't say anything.

*****

I studied the faces of the people as we came down the aisle. "On Eagle's Wings" reverberated through the church. The mass had been painful, but I felt better. It was a fall day and although the sky was blue, it was dreary, like it can be in fall. I noticed weeds in the blacktop across the street as I helped my grandmother into the car.

We drove in procession to the cemetery, moving down side roads; each car had an orange "FUNERAL" sign on the dashboard. At the cemetery, we gathered around the hole dug for the coffin. Cousin José stood across from me. He looked me in the eye and touched his chest twice above the heart, near the outline of his flask. I stared at a giant phallic monument near my grandfather's humble grave. The monument was large. I thought of my grandfather's father, who had been a famous general. We had a letter that had been written to him by President Truman. He died before I was born, and a big funeral was held for him in Miami. There was a parade in his honor and many people were there, including some Masons, to whose fraternity my great grandfather had belonged. My family had been very proud that so many people had honored my great grandfather and attended his funeral. I too had been proud of his memory, but at that moment, it made my grandfather seem less significant. Compared to my great-grandfather's funeral, fewer people had come to bury my grandfather, and the ornaments were smaller and duller. I wondered if my grandfather may have been less of a man than his father. Was it even heroic that my grandfather had escaped Cuba? My great grandfather was in the history books, but no one knew who my grandfather was. We were in Naperville, Illinois, of all places. It wasn't even a city. My grandfather died a carpenter.

When they taught us about Achilles, they told us that he died in a blaze of glory, which had seemed very romantic at the time. I felt nothing but sadness as I struggled to recall my memories of my grandfather. Despite all the days I had spent with him, I could recall very few of them. One memory had weighed heavily on me for days, but I'd pushed it aside.

*****

A priest spoke over the grave of my grandfather. I knew who he was because he had once given a tour me of the monastery. He was fat and ugly, and liked the Black Hawks. He chewed his lip as he spoke, revealing teeth the color of cigarette filters.

My entire life, I had believed in God and Jesus. I even believed that communion was the physical flesh and blood of Christ. As a child, I'd thought that the tabernacle, the golden box in which the Eucharist is kept, was some kind of magical chamber that held the devil. The structure of the church, so daunting, had seemed like a mystical penitentiary, meant to restrain the devil from the world. When I found out that it was not the devil, but the soon-to-be flesh and blood of Christ in that golden box, I felt like a fool. The first time I went to confession, I told the priest my mistake. He gave me a look of horror then had me say six Our Fathers as penance, and three Hail Marys.

Looking at the grass, I slowly realized how much I hated myself, and hated my family for lying to me, and hated my grandfather for dying. He had known full well that he had a heart condition. He had known it all along, and because of his stupidity and his recklessness, we were left out in the cold, my grandmother especially. His death had exposed the entire lie to me, and this obese hockey fan was going to shove the corpse into the earth as if it were some festering insect. I looked at him, chanting like a witch doctor, and the people around me, going through the motions half-heartedly.

There was a terrible smell in the air, and slowly the mourners stopped wiping their eyes with their handkerchiefs and used them to cover their mouths. My forehead grew hot. I felt as if I were going to faint from the smell of dog shit. I fantasized that the priest and I were alone in the graveyard, and I wondered what it would be like to kill him; I that would make me feel better. In my mind, I picked up a shovel and swung it at his skull. He cried out and fell to his knees, bleeding from the mouth. I reached into my pocket and found a pen, which I stuck into his neck. Blood dribbled out like wine, staining my hands. I brought the shovel down onto his face and his neck. By the time I was finished, his face was unrecognizable: a pulp of bloody, moldy bread. It smelled like shit and I gagged.

The last memory I had of my grandfather was of his frightened expression, two weeks before he died. He had been sleeping in his chair when a few of my cousins came over. I had decided I would be funny, so I shrieked in his face while he was asleep. He woke up, startled, and my cousins had laughed raucously. He told me I was a bad grandson. He fell asleep, and then I did it again, and he spoke to me in a hoarse voice. I did it once more, and my grandmother reprimanded me.

¡Ricardo Alonso Campesino! Tú abuelo tiene un heart condition. ¿Quieres matarlo? Porque si quieres, sigue. *Vas a matarlo.*

I looked into the grave. My father's head was buried in the arms of cousin José, whose gaunt face was unmoving. My father held my hand as we walked back to the car in the rain.

*****

Sometime after my grandfather's funeral, I became an atheist. The shock of losing him had shattered any notions of security or happiness that I once had held. Streams of relatives had appeared at our door, but nobody could make me feel protected or certain again. Within my immediate family, my grandfather was only mentioned in praise, or recalled in memory. I couldn't talk about how I felt, and the conversations we had didn't mean anything to me. Whenever I tried to say something, I was greeted with the same platitudes. My relatives reverted to sentiment, and I felt worse than I had before. As if I had eaten nothing for days.

Remember when Uncle Ricardo raised that pig with no ears? My father's cousin Junior recalled after the funeral. What the hell ever happened to that thing?

I think we ate it, someone said.

Roasted pig, ¡Qué delicioso! someone else said. With fried yucca! Tío Ricardo loved fried yucca.

I have a picture of that pig in my office, my father said. Next to the letter from Truman.

*****

There were plenty of salty, roasted memories, but there was little room for questions, which meant that family meals were often silent. I did force my cousin José to have a conversation with me.

Did you cry when you found out? I asked.

Of course. Everyone did, José said.

Don't you wonder if it's all a bunch of lies sometimes?

Lies?

Church and stuff.

I don't go to church anymore. I do my own thing.

So you don't believe in God?

I wouldn't say that. I believe in a higher power, I just don't know if it falls in line with what the church teaches.

What do you mean?

People deal with shit differently. Everyone doesn't necessarily go to church. I got wasted on Jim Beam when I found out Tío Ricardo kicked the bucket. My mother prayed like fifty rosaries; we have to find our own way.

I smashed a picture of San Juan Bosco, I said. José laughed. San Juan Bosco creeps the shit out of me, he said.

A few days after the funeral, I realized that José had been on an airplane at the exact moment my grandfather died. He hadn't come to ask the family for money at a vulnerable time, as my father had said, but had been on his way, as if he had already known it was going to happen. He was the only person who made me feel better during those days, taking me once to the movies, and to Chicago another day. My father didn't like me hanging out with him because he said José was a drug addict. Before José left for the airport, he took me to buy a present. He bought me a Green Day CD called *Dookie*. He said it meant *shit*. That made me laugh. He said it was their best album; I hadn't heard of it. He hoped that the songs would help me deal with the loss of my grandfather.

Naperville Country Club, which is located down the road from the downtown, not far from Benet Academy, was established in 1918. It has only one golf course and an old club house. The Southern-style mansion is white with four tall pillars on a raised deck with a red-carpeted stairway down to the sidewalk. It had bad lighting and the floorboards creaked, but the members did not mind. I had caddied there the summer before, and I had no intention of going back. My most obnoxious employer was a former division-three tight-end. He once chucked a seven-iron after me after a bad shot. I stuck my hands out, but missed the club. The head struck me in the stomach and it dropped pathetically into the rough. The golfer threw two more woods and a sand wedge at me, shouting each time, "Pull it out of the air, boy! Like a man!" I don't like country clubs in general, so when were headed there one Sunday morning, to have brunch with some family friends, I was not pleased. The Fitzgeralds were old family friends who had lived near my family when we first arrived from Cuba. A few of their children had gone to school with my father and uncle.

Why are we going? My sister, Angela, asked as we drove along Washington Road.

Because the Fitzgeralds are close family friends of ours, my father said. And it's been a long time since we've seen them.

If they're such close friends of ours, then why haven't we seen them in such a long time? I asked.

"Don't be a wise-ass." My father said. My mother was putting on eyeliner and looking into the fold-down mirror. She always did that in the car, it drove my father and me crazy. My father slammed it shut.

¡Carajo! ¡No se use el espejo cuando estoy conduciendo!

Richard! She said. Cálmate. The pitch of her voice rose. Why do you always have to yell at me in front of the children? My mother said Reeshard, instead of Richard. My grandmother said it the same way.

Just don't use the damn thing when I'm driving, my father said. You know I hate it. He wiped his palm on his green golf shirt. He breathed heavier and sweat collected at his temples. He complained about how hard he worked, and how lazy we all were. I felt guilty, because some of my friends already had jobs, but my father became so exasperated, that he just turned into a complete snap-job.

Shut up, I said. Stop complaining.

Don't speak to me that way. I'm your father.

Look, neither Angela nor I want to go to this stupid club, but we're going, so stop being a jerk.

Niño! My grandmother said, moving her hand over her mouth, in a gesture of shock.

My father was angry and said nothing more. My mother gave me a disappointed look, but her mouth remained shut. She was wearing a lime-green dress she had bought at Lord and Taylor. I was wearing a red polo. She continued to argue with her husband. My sister, Angela, yelled for everyone to be quiet and Grandma Teresa began muttering under her breath.

This is how I'm spending my twilight years.

*****

Henry Fitzgerald was a burly, freckled man with a large nose. He had many grandchildren and liked to play golf on the weekends. One of cart girls, a blonde named Marlene, smuggled scotch onto the golf course for him at the turn. He paid her in fives. He had been retired for twenty years, having worked in an auto shop, which he was eventually able to purchase due to successful investing. Some property he owned had sky-rocketed in value while he was in his late fifties. He allowed his sons to take the reins at the auto shop, and since then, the Fitzgeralds had been doing quite well.

Lucy Fitzgerald was a large, cheerful woman with a soprano voice. She and my grandmother, Teresa, had been very friendly while their boys were together in high school, and because of this, she sent my grandmother the occasional Christmas card. Lucy was partial to cardigans and loved to play bridge at the club. She wore purple eye shadow and when she met me, she left rouge lipstick on my cheeks. My family and the Fitzgeralds sat at a long table, Mr. Fitzgerald at one end, and my father at the other. Mrs. Fitzgerald asked my mother about Argentina. Mr. Fitzgerald asked Ricky's father how much hair he had on his chest, and then proceeded to order two whiskey sours.

You know, your grandfather was a good man. Mr. Fitzgerald said. I studied his large bespectacled head, and his round glasses.

Thank you, Mr. Fitzgerald. Yes, I know.

Do you know I tried to get your grandfather to invest with me?

No. What do you mean, sir?

I came to him up with an investment plan—IBM and McDonald's. Two of the best stocks I ever bought. Your grandfather, though. He was too conservative for his own good. He thought about it, and then said no. I begged and begged, but I just couldn't get him to do it. You can't win if you don't take a chance." Mr. Fitzgerald's neck wobbled as he continued to talk. Ricky noticed he wore a few rings on each hand. Some had diamonds encrusted in them. "After those stocks took off, boy, every time I saw him I said to him, 'Hey, Rick, how about that IBM! Your grandpa, boy. He was no gambler. He—

My grandmother interrupted him, asking about one of his grandchildren. I was bothered by the stuffy atmosphere. The chairs were stiff and uncomfortable. The table was small; he kept bumping elbows with his sister. He didn't know where to put his hands. Most of the people there were old, but he did recognize a few kids from school, dressed in their Sunday finest. I hated dressing up. I hated wearing dress pants, because I had to wear them enough in school, and I thought golf shirts were for sissies.

Ricky, have you ever seen Blazing Saddles? Mr. Fitzgerald asked me.

No, sir. What is it?

We don't need no stinkin' badges! Mr. Fitzgerald said in an affected accent. He grabbed his stomach and laughed slowly: a-heh, aheh, aheh.

Yeah, my father said, smiling. That was a good one. That Mel Brooks. He's good.

There's that other funny quote. There's a town meeting, you see, Mr. Fitgerald said, breathing loudly. Someone asks who they'll sell land to. And the mayor says, 'Alright, we'll take the niggers and the chinks... but not the Irish!' He knocked on the table and laughed, like he was choking. My father smiled and his mother laughed and touched the hand of Mrs. Fitzgerald, who was apologizing for her husband's language.

Speaking of… Who was that black guy who used to work for us at the plant? Mr. Fitzgerald asked his wife.

Hmm… I don't know. Colt 45?

Coltrane. That's what we called him. Good old, Coltrane.

Oh, I think dad knew him, my father said.

Yup, Coltrane. He was a good one. He was always on time to work, always polite. Coltrane was a good man, Mr. Fitzgerald said, between chews of roast beef. Oh, Richard. Did I tell you what happened to us with the Hartman deal?

Mr. Fitzgerald went into detail over a contract dispute he was moving with a builder. I was confused by the terminology so I lost attention. My mother called the waitress over and asked for a second glass of wine, having to repeat herself because the waitress had not understood her. My grandmother brushed bread crumbs off her black Macy's dress. She looked around the room, wide-eyed.

This is a nice club, no? The people look so nice. She said to me. I nodded. She seemed very impressed. I saw nothing special.

When it comes down to it, Mr. Fitzgerald said, they were just niggers. That's what happens when you do business with them.

I hate to say it, his wife said, nodding, but they were. They were real niggers. Ricky looked at his father. His mouth was open, teeth showing, as if were about to bite something, but he did not look surprised. His grandmother and his mother didn't say anything. His father nodded.

Yup, they were real niggers. Mr. Fitzgerald said again. I played with his unfinished plate of chicken cordon bleu and steamed carrots and asparagus. I eyed looked the untouched "foy's grass" that Mrs. Fitzgerald had ordered as a starter. Mr. Fitzgerald asked me, Do you know what era I grew up in, son?

No, sir.

The Great Depression. I had eight brothers and sisters, and if there was one thing my father taught me, God bless him, it was to lick the plate clean, and be grateful if you had anything to eat. His face became sterner, and the tone of his voice turned dark, You better appreciate where you're sitting. I'm sure your grandfather would have wanted you to.

My tightened my grip on my fork at the mention of my grandfather. Mrs. Fitzgerald slapped her husband's chubby hand and said, Henry! The boy didn't grow up in the Great

Depression. He just didn't like the food. Calm down.

No, he's right, my father said with a self-satisfied look, That's how my father raised me. You should always eat what's in front of you, and be grateful, Ricky. You should take a lesson from Mr. Fitzgerald.

*****

We got into the Explorer, Angela asked my mother about cheerleading in the fall. She said she didn't know, she would have to call Diane's mother to find out. Ricky's grandmother was singing to herself. No one spoke for the first five minutes of the car ride, until Ricky broke the silence.

The Fitzgeralds seem nice, but they're really racist, I said. I could see my grandmother's disapproval by the curve in her eyebrows.

What make you say that? They are nice people.

They said the n-word, I said. Multiple times. Didn't you hear them? Who says the n-word other than black people?

Ricky, that's just how some people talk, my father said.

In Cuba, everyone say 'negro', 'negrito', 'chino', 'chinito'. It does not mean we are racist, my grandmother said.

Yes, it's the same in all of Latin America, my mother said. El presidente de Perú es japonés, pero toda la gente lo llama 'el chino'.

But this is America. You don't say the n-word in English. It's bad. And when he said it! He didn't even look around to see if there were any black people there. My father tensed up. My mother laughed and turned to me.

Ricky, that's because there were no black people there, she said between giggles. Black people at Naperville Country Club. Ha. If you want, I have a friend, Mary, who is black. She plays tennis with me at White Eagle. If you want, I can introduce you to her, you can talk with her. She laughed and rubbed my head. I pushed her arm away.

And he told that joke about 'stinking badges'. I've never even seen that movie and I don't know any Mexicans, either. Does he think we're Mexican?

You know John from tennis lessons last summer? My mother said. I know his mother. He's half-Mexican. See, you do know one.

I didn't even like him. Ricky said.

Ricky, who do you think you are? My father said laughing. Don't you think you're a little young to be making all these judgments?

Dad, don't talk. You changed your name from Ricardo to *Richard.* Immediately his grandmother and mother reprimanded me. My mother told me not to speak like that.

Este niño no tiene respeto para nadie. Diga lo que entre el cerebro, sin pensar. Sin pensar. My grandmother said. My father agreed and began lecturing me. I covered my ears and my sister laughed.

Look, all I'm saying is that the Fitzgeralds are racist. The only reason you're defending them, Dad, is because you're an Uncle Tom.

An uncle what did you say? My father said.

Uncle Tom? Angela said. We don't have an Uncle Tom, his name is Uncle Carlos.

¿Quién es este Tío Tomás? My grandmother said. My father told her to be quiet and there was a lull in the conversation. We ran over a pothole. My sister asked my grandmother if she had an Uncle Tom. His grandmother said she didn't know.

Ricky, my grandmother said. Do you remember the story I told you about your grandfather having a heart attack when your father and your Uncle Carlos were in the high school?

Yeah.

I have to work every day, and your grandfather have to take it easy for two week. Do you know who pick your father and uncle up every day for school? Do you know who bring them back? Do you know who coach Carlos and your father in football? In baseball? In basket? Mr. and Ms. Fitzgerald. They are good people. They helped us when we were so poor your grandpa and I both work six days a week. Don't say bad thing about good people.

I smiled and said, Ms. Fitzgerald coached basket? I'm pretty sure basket-weaving is not a sport, *in this country*.

Mira, nieto. ¡Te voy a dar una galleta!" She raised her hand and my father told her to calm down. My sister began to cry and his father yelled at everyone to shut up. The car became quiet.

Do you know where Mr. Fitzgerald comes from? My father said

The Great Depression? I said.

Mr. Fitzgerald's grandfather was a dirt-poor potato farmer from bum-fuck Ireland. They came over to Ellis Island and lived in a ghetto in New York. Americans treated the Irish like dirt back then. They used to hand signs up saying 'Irish need not apply'. His family didn't come from a background like ours. They weren't wealthy or educated. The reason he uses the n-word so much is because when he was growing up, the Irish were at the bottom, and the only people lower than them were the blacks.

So what's your point? That doesn't make it right.

Ricky, do you know what language the Irish speak?

English, duh.

That's what they speak, now. Duh. Have you ever heard of Gaelic, Ricky? That's the real Irish language. The English conquered them and oppressed them for hundreds of years. By the time they arrived, they'd lost half their culture. They were treated almost as bad the blacks, for many years. Then Jack Kennedy, who was a jerk whose father basically bought him the presidency, got elected and by then the Irish were allowed in. They became white. But today what identity do they have? They've the Chicago River turning green, and South Side Irish and all that crap, but that's not culture, Ricky. That's merchandise. That's green baseball caps for twenty bucks a pop. They may look down on the blacks. They may look down on us. They may look down on the Mexican washing dishes at the club, but they do it, not because the Mexican is poorer or less educated, they do it because they're jealous in their hearts, because they lost their identities a long fucking time ago.

He's right, my mother said, obviously proud of what her husband was saying, and shook her finger at Ricky.

But I don't speak Spanish that well. I said. I'm terrible at salsa-ing; I only know how to merengue a little—

Ricky, you don't realize it right now, but it's there. You understand Spanish. You know about Cuba. You've lived in Argentina when you were young and you've seen parts of South America.

I don't remember any of that! I was born in Chicago and my first memories are from Naperville!

There's a hell of a lot you've seen that these hicks who grew up here in their identical houses will never know or understand. You should be proud of that. My father wasn't talking about history anymore. He seemed angry.

I like Naperville! I like these people! Why are you saying that? Why are you being such a jerk?

I like Yack Kennedy, my grandmother interrupted. And I love Yackie, but her life was so sad. When I live in Cuba, everyone use to say I was chic, like Jackie O.

Quieta, vieja. Estoy enseñándolo algo. Ricky, what's my name?

What? I said, wondering whether my Dad been listening to my rap CDs.

What's my name?

Richard.

What was my father's name?

Ricardo.

What was his father's name?

Ricardo, too. What's your point?

Now, what's your name? My father asked.

Ricardo Alonso Campesino.

That's my point.

Highschool

The first day of high school was uneventful. Ricky wandered through the orientation with his shoulders high, still wearing his football jersey. He met few people that day and tended to stick with his teammates. Benet Academy was an old Catholic Prep school that looked like a red-brick East Coast prep school. It had a long, straight driveway bordered by a ratty metal fence. The campus was always prettiest in the Autumn when school began. The leaves of the maples and oaks lining the long, straight driveway turned red and brown. The rusted fence alluded to the history of the school; it had existed for over one hundred years. The freshmen stared out the window as their mothers and fathers dropped them off in minivans, SUVs, and cars. The upperclassmen pulled in with music playing, uniforms pressed and clean. The temperature dropped slightly and the air became crisp in the morning wind. The students came from various towns in the area.

Jason, tall with spiky hair, said, God, anyone who's not on the football team is a fuckin' pussy.

Fuck yeah, someone said.

The first day was a drag. Moving from class to class, old wooden chair to old wooden chair.

The freshman eyed one another nervously and silently. They tried to give the impression to their peers, and even to themselves, that they were completely nonchalant. Most of the upperclassmen paid little attention to them. These kids look younger and younger every year, a girl on the debate team remarked. Some upperclassmen watched them with smirks. John Randall, a football player, eyed a Barbie-doll freshman as she walked by. She had blonde-streaks in her hair and her skin was the color of tanning oil. She collected looks from most of the boys in the hallway and smiled at John. Across the hallway, Michelle Smith noticed the freshman's facial expression directed at John, her ex-boyfriend. She whispered something into her friend's ear and before the day was over, a third of the school believed that the freshman had herpes. She did, and so did Michelle Smith, but few people knew that.

There was the cantankerous Mr. White, reputed to be the smartest man in the building and head of the English department. With the exception of Mr. Gristokowitz, a feisty, old liberal, the school was composed of recent graduates of Notre Dame. Their heads were far larger than their brains and the students didn't see them so much as teachers as much as devices for vaginal irrigation, of their wives and in the more general sense. The History Department featured a squat bearded man named Mr. Nagis, considered by many to be the best teacher in the school. After school Ricky walked down the steps into the mass of kids, cars, and chatter. He spotted Jason's head above the crowd, and his silver ear ring. He was talking to a girl.

Hey Rick, this is Meghan. She was thin with pouty lips and light brown hair. Rick greeted her calmly, but he was taken with her. She was attractive, with a large, pretty mouth, but it was not obvious, unless one studied her, like a Renaissance sculpture. He noticed her black bra peeking out from under her yellow blouse. Her legs were full, but trim, like an actress's.

Hi, she said. He hesitated and then muttered a hello.

***

He was excited to meet Meghan's sister; they were fraternal twins but he pictured a blonde as beautiful as Meghan. He and Mike stood in front a bench at the movie theatre, waiting. Mike was a Wehrli.

Did you hear about the car crash on Fairview? Mike asked.

No, in Downers or Oak Brook?

Downers. It was a wreck, really ugly. Nobody hurt though.

That's good. Oh, there they are, Rick said, pointing to three girls. Meghan on the left, as stunning as ever in a tube top. He thought the second one was Eileen, but it was Tracy.

Eileen was on the right. She looked like a fourteen year-old Irish step dancer. Big hair. Curly, brunette, and all over the place. She was taller than the other two girls but she didn't look very mature. She had a plain face. He was unimpressed.

***

Hey, what's up? Eileen said as she got into the passenger seat.

Thanks for picking me up. Are we friends yet? Because that would make you my fourth friend here. He laughed. There was something different. Her hair ran down the sides of her face in a deep run. She smiled at him. He was starting to stare. She had a brief shock of a smile. Her mouth made a perfect little triangle, like a cartoon character. On anyone else it would have been packaged and malleable but on her it was as if she had just run all the way down the block, scabs on her knees and grass stains on her jean shorts. It was genuine. Her eyes were knowing and settled into a gentle but beautiful nose. Her legs were her best feature. They were long and thin and copper-colored from a summer spent at the pool. Her sister may have been the star but Eileen was a long-legged goddess living next-door. She was genuine.

No, problem. So where to?

***

Ricky once saw a movie that changed the way her saw himself and his friends. It put foolish ideas in his head. The movie was called Inventing the Abbots, and it starred Jennifer Connolly, Joaquim Phoenix, and Liv Tyler. The movie was set in suburban Illinois and it centered on two brothers from the wrong side of the tracks who courted two girls from the nicer side of town, the Abbot Sisters. He wasn't sure if he had understood the movie completely, but it changed the way he saw the Malloys. Having never touched a football until eighth grade, he put some shoulder pads on and suddenly he was a football player. Having never liked a girl before, he beheld her beauty, and the house she grew up in, and from these things he constructed a fantasy that he was the boy from the wrong side of the tracks. Maybe it was because of this that he decided he would fuck everything up.

Spider Webs

I couldn't remember. It felt like a nest of spiders had settled in my hippocampus, or maybe I was hallucinating.

*****

Sometime after midnight on a Friday, I was driving home from the Caseys' house after smoking cigars with some guys from the football team. I couldn't tell if someone was following me or not, so I kept checking the rearview mirror. My buddy, O'Keefe, knew a Mexican at the country club who smuggled Romeo y Julietas. I threw the remains of a finished cigar onto the side of the road, tasting the bitterness on my tongue and the scent on my hands. I associated smells with places and places with smells. I loved waking up in the morning, to the bitter taste in my mouth and the scent on my fingers. Cigars made me think of my grandfather, even though he never smoked a cigar in his life, neither in Havana, or Naperville. He smoked cigarettes, which I didn't understand. How do you grow up in Cuba and never smoke a cigar? Cigarettes taste like piss. My grandmother had been doing better. She reported the occasional nightmare, but never said more than that. She usually waited up for me on Friday nights, even though my parents went to sleep. There was a trashy Spanish romance novel in the backseat that she had given me. Para ti, mi cielo, she had said. I hated reading in Spanish. There were too many pronouns; I could never understand who the subject was.

*****

Eileen was a funny girl; her middle name was *Macalla*. Her first name was a form of Helen, a name for a beautiful girl. *Eileen Macalla Malloy. I learn my color my lore.* Eileen means *pleasant* in Gaelic, and Macalla means *echo*. *Pleasant echo.* Ella Me Cae Mal. *Echoes of Eileen.* I had many memories of Eileen Macalla Malloy:

I volunteered to pick her up, but she had been indignant.

No, of course not, she said. I can drive myself. We met at the movies on 86th and Stuart Ave. She got out of the car and gave me a hug. She was tall and her arms hung long like rope, locking our bodies together in a hug. She wrapped her arms around my back, locking her hands together. She fit. I held her too long, but I don't think she minded. I drove her around and pointed to landmarks. She wore glasses, which I found endearing.

This is the lake, I said.

Does it have a name? She asked, peeking at me through her sexy librarian glasses.

Not that I know of. They say it's haunted. She rolled her eyes.

I tried to get her to listen to my music but she stuck her tongue out and turned on the radio. She flipped through several stations before pulling a CD out of her purse. I protested but it was hard to say no to her. I actually liked a few of the songs, but I never admitted it to her, at least not for a while. The next time she drove and I got scared and grabbed the dash.

Eileen! I said. You suck at driving.

*****

I asked her to the dance because she was new and didn't have a lot of friends. That's what I told people, that I was just being a nice guy.

*****

The roads were a labyrinth and it was foggy out. Driving back from her house, I went over the infamous night in my mind. Halfway through that night, I had drunk enough to keep my face stuck in a mischievous grin. I was on cloud nine, talking to girls left and right. There were blondes there that night, wrestling in KY jelly, which sounds funny, but if you're drunk and horny, it can fuck with your head. By the end of the night my dick had taken control of my brain, and I tried to put Eileen out of my mind, and succeeded.

I realized the windshield wipers were on, but it wasn't raining. I swore as I turned them off, then my eyes watered. It was hard to see through the glass.

*****

Neither of us had tasted wine before. I wanted to be romantic so I bought a ten dollar bottle of merlot at the 7-11. Our friends had gone to a party in the city but we had been tired. We drank the bottle of Merlot and another of Pinot Gris and watched an old horror film called The Woman from the Lake.

*****

I tried writing poems, which I called *songs,* because that sounded less gay. I used words like "enrapture" and trite phrases such as "furiously in love". The writing was dull and colorless, full of the clichés, but when you wallow in self-pity, everything is tainted, even your sense of taste. My poems, or songs, looked like odd scribbles of Morse Code. Lines of text and dots. I divided every stanza with a sprinkling of asterisks, which served as all-purpose glue, a quick-fix to the question of tying it all together, fastening phrases.

*****

The songs were always the same. So were the places I visited, the old haunts, like the movie theatre and the park. I drove by her house and sometimes I drove around the lake

*****

The first time I tried to kiss her she laughed in my face and said something funny.

This is just like *Friends*, she said. Joey and Rachael try to make out but they can't stop laughing. She spoke the words through giggles and lips. Had it been any other girl my ego would have been deeply wounded, but I found it funny. She hadn't said it to be mean, but had said it because it was funny. I slid my hand under her shirt and she laughed and said, Don't bother, I'm pretty flat

I tried hard not to laugh but I did, and then she kissed me. I felt her breast with my hand and then just the tips of my fingers, for the first and last time.

*****

I burned a few photographs in the bathroom in the basement, the one no one went to. The last photo I burned was a picture of us the morning after formals that my friend Lizzie had taken.

Here's a picture of you and Eileen, Lizzie had said. Oh, shit. I'm sorry I brought it up…

It's all right, I said. Do you think I could keep it?

The picture burned faster than I thought it would, curling up and disintegrating in the flame. I ran the water over the ashes. I jerked off into the sink and ran it again. A spider crawled out of a crack in the ceiling, which I killed it then flushed it down the toilet. I jerked off into the sink and ran the water again.

*****

I called her and told her. She hung up on me and didn't answer after that. I drove all the way to her house, which was half an hour from mine. Meghan answered the door.

She doesn't want to speak with you, she said.

Let me just talk to her, Meghan. Please.

Ricardo, I thought I knew you.

We're still friends right? I asked.

Yeah, we're still friends, Ricky, but Eileen's my sister, my family. She's comes first, Ricky. How could you do this?

Meghan, believe me, I'm sorry. I was drunk—

That's not an excuse. How could you do this? You and Eileen have been inseparable for months and you go to one party with trashy public girls and you turn into a man whore. Even my mom loves you. She always talks about—

What the fuck does that have to do with anything? I said. She gave me a look like my grandmother gave me sometimes and I knew I'd said the wrong thing.

Leave, Ricky. She'll call you later.

Whatever, I thought. There's not much else I can do. I drove to Downers Grove, and met up with my buddies. We had a wicked fun night, shattering lawn gnomes and knocking mailboxes off posts, but I had an uncomfortable feeling in the back of my throat the whole night. Eileen told me it was over a few days later.

*****

In the picture we sat together on bleachers. She wore a black White Sox t-shirt and flip-flops, flashing that same shock of a smile. I wore a ratty t-shirt, smiling dumbly into the camera, but I was obviously happy. My hair was full of cow licks and I had bags under my eyes. At least that's how I remembered it. It had been a long time since I burned the photo.

*****

For the first time in my life I had established a real connection with someone. I wasn't sure if it was love, but I felt a tie to her. Like an invisible thread running from her body into my chest, around my limbs and my neck. It grew warmer and thicker by the day.

*****

I was at the Central party, I said. I don't remember. I was drunk.

Who was the girl? She asked.

I don't know. Whatsername. What does it matter?

It matters, she said.

Eileen, I said. The line went dead.

*****

We lay in bed. She touched the scar on my hand.

Where did you get this? She asked. It looks like you sliced open your hand.

You gave it to me, don't you remember? I said.

What are you talking about? She asked. Maybe she was right. Maybe I was hallucinating.

*****

She was extremely charismatic, despite the fact that she seemed to have grown up in her sister Meghan's shadow. Meghan was gorgeous, no one doubted that, but then Eileen walked into class on a Monday morning, everybody knew about it, because she was so friendly, and charming, and you gave her a week or two and she'd probably paint a little sign for the teacher or make him a little box for people to turn in homework. And not because she was a teacher's pet, she was just funny that way. She did that kind of stuff without being nerdy, or at least not caring what other people thought, which I loved. When we were first dating, she had very few friends. I had liked the fact that I had her to myself, but I knew it wasn't the best for her.

*****

We remained friends afterwards. She called me one night because she was worried. Something about the guy she was hooking up with.

After we had sex—

You lost your virginity to him? I asked. She laughed for what seemed like too long a time.

What is it with guys and virginity? She asked. I'm a grown woman. I've been hooking up with this guy on and off for the last four months. I can make my own deci—,

I'm sorry. It's none of my business. I'm going to go, and I hung up before she could say anything else. It had been over a year since we broke up, but I still broke into my parent's liquor cabinet. I poured some Jack Daniels into a blue Solo cup, then put the bottle under the faucet and replaced what I'd taken. I mixed in some Coke, but we didn't have much, so it still tasted like shit. I didn't feel any better after the drink, so I went running in the rain later that night. I ran four miles. The next time I saw her, she offered me a remorseful smile in the hallway, and I shot one back like my yearbook photo. Later that week, I got a blow job from Grace Johanssen, arguably the hottest girl in the school, and arguably the hottest girl I ever pulled. I came all over Grace's tits, but I didn't feel any better about myself. The guy who fucked Eileen was a fucking loser.

*****

A beautiful web, I thought, but where was the spider? Where was the prey? I had always hated spiders. Disgusting things, spinning webs. Bloated thoraxes and legs that shiver after death. Every time I killed one, it seemed another would come and replace it.

I could see a faint reflection in the spaces between the lines of the web, a reflection of Eileen's face. I was stuck to the web. Staring at her reflection, I realized she must be behind me, but I couldn't turn to see if she was actually there. This weighed heavily on me mind; I just wanted to turn to see if he was there, but I couldn't move my neck all the way around. I was tied down to the web and I still didn't know where the spider was. I noticed there was some froth on her mouth, as if she had been drinking beer. I realized then that it wasn't froth by eggs on the web itself; they weren't a part of her reflection. Frothy eggs stuck to the web.

This was a recurring dream. One day at school, after having thought about the dream, I realized that I might be the spider.

*****

She had been wasted at that first dance. I took care of her and walked her to the car. She started making out with me in the backseat, which my friends thought was hilarious. I had never seen her like that. She was really drunk. She had been chugging a bottle of vodka. I told my friend to watch the road.

*****

That first day of school I asked her to come to my house. She had been hesitant at first, but then she agreed and followed me home. She wore her uniform skirt and we played Frisbee in the park with my collie. She had nice legs and grass stains on her knees. We started dating after that. I liked that memory.

*****

When I thought of her, the lines evaporated; her kisses were like the last sips of soft drinks. I realized that so much time had passed that the Eileen I'd been in love with wasn't even the same person anymore. She had had every right to dump me, but in the last few months, she'd become a different person. She was a slut.

*****

This always happens to me, she said. This exact thing happened at my old school, except my best friend blew the guy in my car. I'm not going to be the laughing stock again, Ricky. I can't trust you.

*****

An Irish flute swooned as the credits began to roll. I looked over at her. She was lying on her back with her hands folded across her stomach. Her hair hung down the sides of her face and fanned out like threads. I rubbed a hickey on my neck that she had given me. I leaned over her and pressed my mouth to her long, thin Irish lips. She woke up and I said goodnight.

*****

My memories bled into one another as I hung in that vodka-soaked limbo. I saw the color of his grandmother's bathrobe, but couldn't make out the lines. I couldn't distinguish her face; all I could see were the age spots on her olive skin. My mouth tasted bitter, of blood or tobacco and I needed to pee. I touched my penis and realized there was a catheter in me. They found me a ditch near a party on a Friday night; my blood alcohol level was .35. I was bleeding from my temple and had slit open my hand on broken glass. Upon waking in the hospital, I felt suffocated by the medical cords coming out of me. I hated them and I hated the feeling of being stuck in a bed. My grandmother looked down on me. I flexed my right hand, which was bandaged, and turned my head. My neck was sore. There were various medical cords attached to me. An IV ran across my body like a rope. My grandma checked to see that it was still connected to my arm; earlier in my sleep I had ripped it out of the vein.

You look like your grandpa, she said.

Where are my clothes?

Your parents are flying home from Phoenix. Your sister saw you but don't worry. I tell her you have food poisoning from T.G.I. Friday.

I became a rat during the summers. A gym rat. A book rat. I wanted to start on Varsity at safety so I hit the weight room three times a week. I ripped the sleeves off all my t-shirts. I went shirtless when the sun was out. I wore sleeveless t-shirts I ran sprints on the track around the football field. I wore sleeveless t-shirts to bed. Or nothing at all. I became a gym rat during the summers.

Monday

Pre-workout shake: NO-Xplode (creatine,caffeine,guaraná, gasoline... [it gives a lot of guys the shits, but it's a good pump-up]). Two cups of water. Banana. Fifty minute drive to Benet from my house, listened to Zeppelin the whole way. Hit the locker room, drop my bag off, leave my sandals in the locker and put on some running shoes. We had workout partners but I usually worked out by myself. Squats. Stretch out hammies, quads, lower back, and inner thighs. Loosen your shoulders by doing some arm circles. Ten warm-up reps at 135. Ten reps at 225 pounds. I'm OK. Eight reps at 265. My gluteus maximus is starting to feel it and my adductors feel like rope. Six reps at 290 pounds. I love it. Some of the lineman scrubs have shown up. They're loud and stupid, and they suck at football, and they can't squat as much as I can, even though I'm a defensive back, but I enjoy their company. Burts tells a story about finger-banging a freshman. She had acne. They put on Journey (I fucking hate Journey), but it's good to sing along to in the weight room. I'm a quiet guy anyway. I'm not going to complain. Six reps at 315 pounds. I touch the red welt that has developed on the skin over one of my vertebrae. Where the squat bar rests. My legs are massive. One more rep to go and I can move on to my next exercise. Four reps at 345 pounds. One. I didn't even get half-way down on that one. My lower back feels like a twig. About to snap. Two. I get a little farther down, but I can't feel my hamstrings anymore. Three-- I lose control and bail out of the squat. Fuck. The bar crashes down onto the safety rods and thunder deafens the weight room. Everyone looks at me but doesn't say shit. My friend Grant Casey, hung-over and just arrived, says, Take it easy Campesino. It's Monday. No need to show off. Fuck off, Casey.

After that, I did squat thrusts, quads, hammies, adductors, and abductors. I drank two big plastic water bottles full of water. I finished up with a two mile jog and abs. I was at Benet a total of five hours. I'm still pissed off I didn't finish my last set. By bedtime, I had drank two more protein shakes, with 30 grams of protein each (two scoops whey powder, chopped up banana, peanut butter, crushed ice, skim milk. Delicious). And ate a few small meals which consisted of egg whites, chicken breasts, a handful of nuts, some celery, carrots perhaps, maybe an apple or two, maybe some Cheerios. And more water. Athletes need protein and water. Especially if you're taking creatine supplements

During the summer, athletes tend to work out all day, then either go to their jobs (lifeguarding at pools, or teaching younger kids how to play sports) or go home and watch DVDs or play Halo. We didn't drink as much as they portray it in the movies. Alcohol takes a lot out of you, especially after 3 hours weight-lifting, an hour of jogging, and another hour of shooting the shit with your boys. Maybe a quick conversation with one of the freshman pieces. Cheerleaders. Gotta love 'em. My whole life I'd had trouble falling asleep, so when I came home from these workouts, I usually took short naps, as opposed to sleeping the whole day, like most of my teammates. We didn't have many DVDs in my house, and I got sick of going to Blockbuster or Hollywood Video. So I read a lot. On Mondays I read Hemingway. Because my grandparents had partied with him once or twice (or maybe never at all, who knows?), my father had purchased every novel, nonfiction work, and collection of short stories with the name Hemingway on it. And I mean, shit.

He was from Illinois and he wrote about Cuba. Talk about a writer I was meant to be interested in. In fact, he won the Nobel Prize for Literature, *for writing about Cuba.* Cheap Christian imagery, my ass. I liked it.

Despite the fact that I was predestined to read his stuff, I didn't see what the big deal was about the guy. I mean, OK. Some of his novels were pretty cool. The whole tough guy thing. Lots of strong drink, and not many feelings, but the shit gets repetitive after a while. I mean don't get me wrong. Some of his shit was fierce, especially the end of A Farewell to Arms, where the chick dies with the guy's baby or whatever. And Hemingway ends the book with: *After a while I went out and left the hospital and walked back to the hotel in the rain.* I had to put the book down, I was so shaken. Talk about cold. *After a while I went out and left the hospital andwalked back to the hotel in the rain.* That's some cold fucking shit.

Tuesday

Tuesdays were for improving speed, quickness, agility, explosiveness, and football intelligence. We played 7 on 7, too, which was probably one of the few things we did which were actually fun. I woke up a half hour earlier than on Mondays and stretched immediately, because my legs were shot from squats. I ate cheerios with milk, and some egg whites and orange juice. I drove to the Speed Clinic and met some of my other teammates. We began with stretches, then moved to pliometrics, focusing on our form. Quick feet. Full extension. Explosiveness. Perfection. Beat the other guy. After that, we headed over to the fields behind the school to run 7-on-7. Linebackers and DBs versus Backs, receivers, and the tight end (depending on the offensive scheme). 5 yard outs.

Posts. Flags. The occassional hook-and-go if they were feeling cheap. Arms hanging. Eyes flipping back and forth between the quarter back's eyes and the your primary receiver's hips. Watch the fakes. Jam him at the line of schrimmage. Tomahawk the ball. Rip it out. Or just intercept the damn thing. Run it back, flip the ball at the offense. Afterwards, jog a mile to get the acid out of the legs. Repeat the protein shakes. Ice bath to keep the legs fresh. I tried to reread The Great Gatsby but passed out before the Gatz got offed.

Catcher in the Rye was my favorite book of adolescence. Like so many other angst-ridden brats, I, too, identified with Holden Caufield, whom my friend Peter once called the most charismatic character in all of literature. I ignored the top-layer differences that separated me and Holden. The fact that he was a boarding school kid and that he grew up on the upper east side of Manhattan, whereas I was Chicago-born. I empathized with him because all he wanted to do was protect people. He had no time for phonies. Although I couldn't understand why he didn't give it up to that whore. My English teacher Mr. White taught the book in class, and opened up all the hidden meanings and symbols. The red hat. The ducks at the pond. The nuns. All that jazz. It made me love the book even more.

I read the Lord of the Rings in six days, all 1000+ pages. I loved every minute and I had to take an hour long break after Frodo and Gandalf sailed into eternity. I devoured Joyce's Dubliners. The writing was logical and easy to understand, and I felt satisfied after every single story. I particularly identified with the boy's tears at the end of Araby, and was distraught over Eveline's decision to stay in Ireland.

Wednesday

My alarm went off at seven a.m. sharp. Orange-flavored pre-workout shake. Caffeine. Sugar. Protein. Gasoline. Sat at the table with my dad as he sipped coffee before work, listening to NPR. It took me fifteen minutes to get to Benet that day. AC/DC's black album echoed out my open windows. Bench warm-up. Ten reps at 135 pounds. Spot McAvoy on the incline bench then return to the flat bench. Six reps at 195 pounds. My chest muscles were tight. Fill up a water bottle and drink a third of it. Six reps at 215 pounds. My hands were calloused. Five reps at 225 pounds. My triceps burned. Final set. Five reps at 235 pounds. Repeat with Decline bench. Flys. Military press. Protein shake at noon. Two scoops with well water. (Mmm... Taste the minerals) Pickup basketball afterwards. My first shots bricked against the glass. My arms felt like pieces of wood, so I stuck to layups after that.

I never finished Frank Miller's the Dark Knight because I didn't have the patience to read all the dialogue bubbles, and look at each and every frame. However, after studying it for an hour or so, I quickly understood why it was considered one of the greatest comic books of all time. Miller took Batman, the darkest and most flawed of the popular superheroes, and made him even darker. The Batman of the Dark Knight was a tough, old son of a bitch. He had more in common with a medicated Vietnam vet then a superhero. Miller was even able to make Superman, the blandest of all superheroes, a little bit interesting. In one part of the comic book, Superman carried a nuclear weapon, which subsequently detonated. The subsequent frames show a skeleton with an S on its chest and baggy clothing. The frame that will forever be in my mind showed a wounded Batman next to the corpse of an eerily-smiling Joker.

Thursday

Egg whites have about 3 grams of protein per egg. Lots of eggs whites. No yolks. Skim Milk. Cheerios. Pre-workout energy shake. Tasted like raspberries and sourcream. Water. A whole lot of water. My legs and back ached when I got out of bed. My pectorals and deltoids were tight. My muscles burned. The warm joy of achievement. I listened to the Best of Ray Charles on my way to the Velocity workout facility. My favorite song was Georgia on My Mind. We began by walking through hurdles, making sure to stretch our hips out, which the instructor assured us, was the best way to develop playmaker speed. We did skips in order to increase the explosive power of our calf muscles. We jumped onto boxes in order to maximize the explosiveness of our calf muscles. We ran sprints back and forth on the artificial turf in order to control the explosiveness of our calf muscles. More protein shakes. Tasted like watermelon and old sandwiches.

Another school came to visit us for 7 on 7. St. Francis. They used to be our rivals but they were moved to the shitty league and they suck balls. Coach put in the number 2s after twenty plays, and then we grilled out by the baseball fields. I had two picks. New had six. Norfenweiler ate five cheeseburgers.

Reading Swann's Way was like trying to cut through a flower bed with a tooth brush. It was impossible. I read two-hundred pages and all I could remember was that at one point a madelaine had been bitten. And I got that from the book jacket. Thank God I didn't try to read it in French.

Friday

My favorite book was Tim O'Brien's The Things They Carried. I loved the way he wrote. It was easy to understand on the immediate level, yet so rich and full of meaning. The characters were unforgettable. Bowker. Rat Kiley. The girlfriend that became a Green Beret. The opening chapter is some of the best writing I've ever read in my life. I loved the metaphor of "carrying". *They carried football helmets and Dave Matthews concert tickets and hitters and dip cans and rosaries. They carried text books, crushes, disorders, and lip gloss. They carried the weight of the Catholic Church on their shoulders. They carried the weight of what it was to be young and in the western suburbs of Chicago. These were the things they carried.*

*****

Third down. One minute on the clock.

Minooka. Minooka. I called out. Hawk left. Hawk left. As the strong safety, it was not only my job to make plays but to call out the formation and set up the defense. I was one-on-one on a speedy tight-end who already had a touch down that game. The ball was spiked and I jumped into my back pedal. The left guard pulled. It was a sweep to the right. The end came right at me, much faster than I thought. Pass. Pass, I yelled. I twisted my hips in an effort began sprinting with him, but I wasn't quick enough. I heard my own labored breath, and felt the ulcer in my gut as they end stayed two steps ahead of me. I tried to slow him down with my left arm, but he was too good. Too quick. You can lift all th weights in the world, but that still won't make you quick. How much time had passed? 3 seconds? 7 seconds? Had the quarterback thrown the ball? I turned my head back to look. It was sailing through the air. A perfect spiral. I looked back at my man. Then at the ball. Then at my man. I moved my running line a little to the left, thinking it would bring me closer to the ball. We both jumped, and he swuing his hips into me. I reached for the ball and tipped it out of his hands. I hit the ground and I couldn't see anything but grass, mud, and the outline of my helmet. The crowd erupted. The fucker had caught it. The stoppage before the field goal delayed the inevitable. The ball skirting through the uprights. Benet 20. St. Pat's 21.

*****

I was 5'10 and 165 pounds when I arrived at Benet Academy in the fall of my freshman year. By the beginning of football season my senior year, I was 5'11, 185 pounds, and could run a 4.78 forty. My squat max 380 pounds (tied with a starting d-tackle for the best on my team). My bench max was 270. Our season was a complete failure. We went 3-8 and I played like shit in seven of the games. After our last game, a trouncing of St. Joes's (a basketball school. Isaiah Thomas went there. Derek Rose just came out of there), I walked back to my car, wondering what Eileen was doing. She had dumped me two months before. Fuck, I thought. I should have juiced.

Are you crying? I asked. Her mascara streaked like ashes.

No, of course not.

Mom, you're crying. What's wrong? Did something happen?

No, no. Everything's fine.

Mom, I'm not an idiot. I can see the tears on your face. Did someone die?

Yes, my brother.

Oh. I'm sorry…I don't think I ever met him.

You met Ernesto when you were young. Everyone says you look just like him.

How did he die? I held her hand, running my finger over her soft skin, right where the fingers connect to the hand, the knuckles. My mother was the reason we still went to Buenos Aires. She had left all of her family and friends to raise me in Chicago.

***

Telling people that I was going to spend Christmas in Buenos Aires always sounded more exotic than it was. I was "going to visit my mother's family", I would add tentatively. Surely my friends imagined crimson tangos, poems written over Malbec wine, and long-haired brunettes with bits of *dulce de leche* on their lips.

I never saw that part though. My knowledge of Buenos Aires extended to the doldrum drive from the airport. The smaller stick-shift cars. That extra layer of filth or grease that seems to collect over the streets of Latin America. The poverty. Las villas miserias. Kids with sun-darkened skin and a pair of underwear, wandering the streets, swimming in fountains, and stealing a peso from your mother when she buys a coffee. I felt guilty for the way we lived. Buenos Aires, to my friends at home, was different, exotic. Yet to me, it was musty old apartments. No tangos, no salsas. No, I could not dance very well. It was the stench of dust and ancient decadence that layered my maternal grandparents' apartment. I had never known my uncle Ernesto. I had known of him of course, because everyone reminded me that he had indeed existed. That he had indeed loved me very much. My mother often reminded me of the love of the dead. Every family, even happy families, has its own secrets. Most are buried with the dead, but I met a live one. She was a year younger than him with caramel skin and eyes like gems. Her name was Encarnación. She was the bastard child of my uncle, dead two years.

The wilting photographs on the wall of the old apartment had hinted at a handsome rugby player, a fly-half. Ernesto. He had been an excellent marksman as well; he could have competed in the Olympics for Argentina, but he had enjoyed guns enough to put down the bottle.

***

I learned to speak Spanish in Argentina. I was bored most of the time, and one day I found a Castilian translation of Dostoesvky's The Brothers Karamazov, circa 1920. I went through it like a little monk, transcribing it with the help of an old English-Spanish dictionary that had belonged to my mother. I was halfway through the speech of the Grand Inquisitor when a package arrived from Naperville. It was full of comics: Dilbert, Calvin and Hobbes, and Garfield. Grandpa Ricardo had sent it.

***

Please help us to fight the War on Terror. Report any suspicious ~~activities.~~ A-RABS

We advise you to be watchful

Current Warning Level: RED

Department of Homeland Security

I finished reading the sign and returned to waiting in line to check my baggage. Angela was listening to her Ipod, and my father was to his right, sweating and clutching: three tickets, three passports.

This is ridiculous. You would think that they would have figured out a better way to deal with this.

Deal with what? I asked. There was only one person ahead of us in the customer service line. My father was a frequent flyer and a 1K member, so they had not even had to wait in the longer line for coach passengers.

With everything… My father replied, his watch ticking impatiently. They need to be more efficient with customer service, with the luggage, with everything. My father was referring to the uncertainty over when their flight would take off. I felt that it was best not to worry about these things, especially at airports. It was not worth it. I was also quite relaxed on account of the two cans of Guinness I had finished before we had reached O'Hare.

After checking in and passing through a metal detector, we stood together, dressing ourselves as a family. My father looped his belt as if he had but a minute to live, pulling his pants up, around his girth.

Angela! Please take your Ipod off! My father said. Angela looked at my father with a look of incredulity.

Dad, for the millionth time, what is the difference?

Why do you have a beard? My father asked me. Are you trying to make a statement?

No… I said. I didn´t understand why my father cared. He had had a mustache since the age of twenty two. I'm home from college, I said, and I don't feel like shaving every fourteen hours to keep my face smooth.

You look like a terrorist.

Yeah, that makes a lot of fucking sense.

Look, Angela, I said, pointing at a fat guy. That guy's a terrorist. She laughed. Then I pointed to another man with a goatee, his hair was blue. Look, Angela. Another terrorist.

Shut up, that's not funny. My father said.

You're doing that Dick Cheney thing again, my sister said. She slipped one of the headphones off.

What?

That thing where you talk out the side of your mouth. You always do that in airports. It's creepy.

Yeah, Dad, I said. She's right.

Maybe I only do it when I'm stressed.

Well don't do it anymore, Angela said. It's creepy.

The first time I hooked up with Eileen was at a party in the city. Her older brother, a Benet grad, was a student at DePaul and he let her invite a bunch of people down to his house in the city. We weren't dating yet, but I had kissed her on the cheek a few nights before and we called one another frequently. It was the winter, and since I had quit basketball after sophomore year, I didn't have to worry about games or practice. I sneaked into my parents liquor cabinet, cooked up some white russians, and fantasized that I was the Dude. I slipped on a t-shirt and dirty jeans, and rocked out to some Creedence (CDs, not tapes), until my friends came for me.

Cole Barrett had a shit-eating grin. He had a shit-eating grin, offers to play quarterback for Butler and Valparaiso, and a Ford F-150. Cole was a good friend of mine. Washing out the bourban glass, I checked myslf in the mirror, and sprayed myself with an old bottle of Ralph Lauren cologne that had belonged to my grandfather. Cole knocked on the door and greeted my mother and grandmother, who were both delighted to see him. He was a favorite of the Benet Mother's Club.

Make sure he don't drink the alcohol, Cole, my grandmother said.

Don't worry, grandma Camps, Cole said. I'll look after him. The Delarosa twins, Grant and Gerry, were in the backseat, giggling like idiots.

What up, biatches, I said. Cole put on Get Low by Lil' John and the Eastside Boys. I don't know if it was the alcohol, or the excitement about going to a party in Chicago, but we sang along, waving our hands, as if we were costars in some terrible chick flick. After a while, I switched on the new Ying Yang Twins album and watched the lights go by.

Did you hear Craig and two other seniors ran a train on Stacie D'Abuzzo? Grant asked.

Don't listen to him, Gerry said. He's high as shit.

I don't know if I believe you Grant, I said. But if that's true, that's the funniest shit I've heard all day.

You guys are terrible, Cole said. Stacie's a nice girl. She's my friend. Cole had been secretly hooking up with Stacie for the last four months. He thought no one knew about it, and few people did, except for all our friends, including Grant, Gerry, and I.

You would say that, Cole, Gerry said. You were probably there giving Craig a reacharound.

Yeess, Cole said in a funny accent. I like very much.

We got lost and were driving around Chicago. We drove down lake shore drive, (and in no particular order) by Belmont Harbor, Soldier Field, Rogers Park, Evanston, and over the Chicago River. We were fucking lost. Finally we got to the party. Two dudes were drinking beers on the porch. Pabst Blue Ribbon. One had a shaved head with a tattoo of a snake on his neck, and the other had dreadlocks. Gerald knew one of them so he stayed on the porch as we made our way in, sliding through the wash of familiar faces.

I think I went to volleyball camp in grade school with that kid, I said.

You went to volleyball camp? Gerry asked. Ha. Fag.

I won the vertical jump award. I still have the t-shirt. I fell into conversation with a cute blonde on the volleyball team named Julie. I knew she liked me because of the way she touched my arm when we spoke. She played the position that wears the off-color jersey; her ass looked like heaven in spandex.

Eileen's shirt looked like a short dress, but she was wearing jeans underneath. It annoyed me when girls did that, because it made them look pregnant.

I hung out with Mary and Lisa today, she said.

Who are Mary and Lisa? I asked.

My friends from gradeschool. You met them, silly. We sat down on old red velvet couch with beer stains, and talked for a long time. The conversation was vapid and unimportant; full of pauses like on television. She was chewing sugarless gum, because she still had braces on at that point. I slid my hand behind her back to let her now that I liked her. I held it there and she kissed my forehead. Her kiss was warm. We played flippycup for an hour and then sneaked into her brother's vacant bedroom.

On the way home from the city the next day, we were hung over as shit.

My feelings were written plain on my forehead, for everyone to see. We had all been gone for some time, but who had changed? Who had stayed the same? I wore glasses and an old black LaCoste shirt, but I was regretting it, then. I felt like I was being judged. I spied Eileen immediately. Her long brown hair, and that familiar shock of a smile. She greeted me with drunken, child-like stare. Her cheeks looked swollen and her clothes tight. I was over her, but I couldn't help feeling a small bit of satisfaction at the thickening of her thighs. The roundness in her face. The kiss of Keystone Light. I decided to avoid her.

Friends caught up with one another. We hugged and pretended to be as happy as we had been in the last month of school, when we had gathered on third baseline to cheer for Benet Baseball. We had grilled burgers and taken lippers, listened to Dave Matthews Band and Bone Thugs, and enjoyed the freedom of not having to give a shit about anything other than the score. The girls had worn skirts, Sox t-shirts, ball caps, and pony tails. The guys wore whatever. That had been the best of times, before that summer. The last summer. Before everyone had had it out for everyone else. Someone tapped me on the shoulder.

Ricky! How are you?

Good. How about you? I couldn't remember her name.

Wonderful. I just got back from Europe. She proceeded to list off some cities and I nodded my head mechanically. Why they hell am I here, I thought. Before I could think of an answer, one of my friends approaced with two beers, carved up like jack-o-lanterns. His voice was two octaves lower than I remembered it. He was inebriated. I followed him to the dining room where I took some shots with friends. Bacardi 151. We played games together.

Twenty minutes later, I wandered off, looking for newer, more attractive people to talk to. I walked haltingly, like Frankenstein's monster, swaying back and forth to the melody of imaginary music. Two of my friends were fighting.

Go fuck yourself you fat little slut.

Go to hell, asshole.

Why don't you go suck someone off? The girl scurried off, followed by two of her friends, carrying cellphones, and bottles of Smirnoff Ice.

Fuck yeah. You tell that slut what the fuck is up, someone shouted.

I went to see how the girl was. She was lying on the bed, crying, with two of her friends. I proceeded to hug her and say things that I didn't mean.

All those things he said were a bunch of lie, I said. Don't listen to him.

I know. I know. It just hurts, you know? I hugged her and felt good about myself.

Ricky's right, said one of her friends. As I walked down the stairs, I thought I heard one of her friends ask, Did he just try to hook up with you?

Fat slut, I muttered under my breath. I stumbled down the stairs to the basement, landing on my ass. The guys were yelling. One of them picked up a photo and chucked it against the wall.

What the fuck are you guys breaking shit for? Someone asked.

I dunno, the guys said, laughing.

What were you fighting about? I asked the guy who had made the girl cry.

That slut told my girlfriend that I cheated on her. They aren't even friends. What the fuck business is it of hers to go around talking about other people's shit? His friend chimed in with an emphatic, Yeah, every once in a while.

That's bullshit, I said. I can't believe she would do that. You gave her what she deserved, man. After a few testosterone-filled minutes of shooting the shit, I crawled up the stairs, feeling quite sick, but not because of the alcohol.

A door was ajar, across the hallway and to the left. I walked toward it, slowly and deliberately,knowing full well what lay behind it. I peeked in. I saw a backwards facing New York Yankees cap and some guy straddling what looked like a someone on a chair. To the left of the cap, I saw half of that familiar face, with the long brown hair. The Yankees cap blocked most of Eileen's face, including her mouth, but she opened her right eye. It met me with an honest look and the pupil expanded slightly upon recognition.

Part 2: An American Fury

I will do such things
What they are yet I do not know—
but they shall be
The terror of the earth

King Lear

Ricky was hungover. He had stars in his eyes. Cotton ball-shaped flashes of silver and light that come after a long night of revelry. A passed out by 5 am night of balls to the wall. A pissfest that started out well enough with crushed cans of shitty beer in the dorm. Boilermakers (beer and a shot of Yäeger) in water bottles on the way to the Mansion Club. Tequila shooters at early hours and vomit in the urinal.

It was a fun night; he had danced with Taylor Cordenay and taken her home. She was an oil-bronzed bombshell on the soccer team who played hard-to-get. Her beauty and her her body were rare at a school like Princeton; he was proud. Yet despite the conquest, he was disconcerted.

His eyeballs ached and he felt annoyed with everyone around him. He was depressed as well, which worried him. His greatest assurance in life was that no matter how shitty and terrible he might feel during the night hours, he always awoke with a disposition colored by an adamant hope, a kind of audacity that he believed unique. He never felt this way after a night of revelry. He knew his drinking was affecting his life, but he didn't know how to stop, short of renouncing pleasurable habits. His grades were fine. He was playing shitty rugby, but he was having fun. He was weary, but instead of addressing himself, he was cold to everyone around him…

Y despues de toda la mierda que pasó. Habia los trés amigos. Los trés caballero andantes. Los tres *poet warriors*.

GLEASON

CABRERA

MCLAIN

DICIERON VETE A LA MIERDA A TODOS Y SE FUERON A ARGENTINA……..

Y se metieron en un lío.

www.ingramcontent.com/pod-product-compliance
Lightning Source LLC
Chambersburg PA
CBHW020614310726
48979CB00008B/1483/J

* 9 7 8 0 6 1 5 2 2 2 8 5 1 *